Mystery at
BLACK ROCK ISLAND

Robert Sutherland

Cover by Laurie McGaw

Scholastic-TAB Publications Ltd.,
123 Newkirk Road, Richmond Hill, Ontario, Canada

Canadian Cataloguing in Publication Data

Sutherland, Robert, 1925-
    Mystery at Black Rock Island

ISBN 0-590-71151-2

I. Title.

PS8587.U83M97   jC813'.54   C83-094137-1
PZ7.S87My

Copyright © 1983 by Robert Sutherland. All rights reserved. No part of this publication may be reproduced in whole or in part, or stored in a retrieval system, or transmitted in any form or by any means, electronic, mechanical, photocopying, recording or otherwise, without written permission of the publisher, Scholastic-TAB Publications Ltd., 123 Newkirk Road, Richmond Hill, Ontario, Canada L4C 3G5.

1st printing 1983   **Printed in Canada**

Mystery at
BLACK ROCK ISLAND

For my family,
especially Ruthie

1

A sound—vague, all but indistinguishable. Perhaps, after all, just imaginary.

David hesitated. He hunched deeper into his collar and peered about him into the mist. This must be what they call "Scotch mist," he reflected. Rain, really—not a good, steady, pelting rain, but a fine, silent, soaking blanket.

That sound again. Just a sea gull if anything, its cry distorted by the mist.

The vapour had swept in swiftly and silently, blotting out the southern Hebrides scattered across the sea. The surf washed in to the white sand at his feet as if from nowhere. Above him the cliff top had melted and vanished. The cliff itself was just a darker shade of grey in a grey world.

There it was again! Half moan, half cry.

David shivered. Old tales of highland superstitions suddenly flashed across his mind—tales of strange, malignant creatures from some subterranean world. Anything was believable in a world like this where, in moments, warm sunshine became a clammy shroud.

He stopped still, listening intently. Where had the sound come from? Not from the sea. There was nothing out there except a foghorn now and then sounding its lonely dirge. David peered into the mist, trying to recall his surroundings. Behind him sand stretched as far back as the river mouth. Ahead of him it reached to a rocky promontory some distance away. On his left lay a sheer rock wall with a straggle of undergrowth at its base. That must be where the sound originated.

Then he heard it once more and this time there was no mistaking it. "Help!" The word was distinct--a cry of despair, a low cry somewhere near at hand.

It had to be from the cliff. David turned and moved ahead until the grey cliff solidified and undergrowth clutched at his ankles.

"Where are you?"

"Here."

To his right. David groped forward, his hand out to feel the wet face of the cliff. Then he found and knelt down beside a crumpled shape at his feet. One arm was flung wide, one leg bent horribly, the face white, a scarlet thread of blood at the corner of the mouth.

"Oh, no!" Instinctively David looked up to where the cliff vanished in the mist overhead. Could anyone survive a fall like that? He groped for the man's wrist to search for a pulse.

The eyes flickered open, pain-filled eyes. The lips moved soundlessly.

David struggled out of his coat and wrapped it around the man. "I'll get help," he said. "I don't dare move you. There's a hotel not too far away—"

"No!" The word exploded. "Too late!"

David wanted to get away, to find capable help, but a conviction that it *was* too late stayed him. If he could give the man a little comfort...

"Listen." There was a plea in the eyes and voice.

David leaned closer to the man's lips. For a moment there was no sound. Then, with great effort, the words came, slowly and distinctly.

"Paper in my right boot...must be delivered to man in Tobermory...Friday...noon boat."

The voice weakened, but its urgency was contagious.

"Who? Who is he?"

The eyes flickered, became vacant, then focused again. David could sense the effort in the tautening of the shattered body. "Badge...under collar...know you by that." The voice stopped. The eyes closed.

David's trembling fingers moved under the collar of the man's shirt. There. It was a feather, a gull's feather, stuck into a brooch that depicted the rampant lion of Scotland. He fumbled with the clasp and took the brooch and feather off.

The eyes opened again. "You will...see he gets it?"

David heard a desperate urgency in the fading voice. The eyes, suddenly wide open, held his. He nodded.

The eyes closed. The lips relaxed, releasing a new trickle of blood.

David crouched there, his mind a turmoil.

What on earth had he stumbled onto? Why hadn't he just been given the *name* of the mysterious man in Tobermory? Why a gull's feather as identification? And why an important paper in a boot of all places?

Oh, yes, the boot.

Thank goodness the right leg was not the one that was so horribly bent. He found a knife pouch on the calf of the boot but no paper tucked inside. The boot lace was leather, the wet knot so tight his fingers couldn't loosen it. He tried using the tip of the blade.

Suddenly a long, shuddering sigh shook the body. Then it was still, absolutely still.

He's dead, thought David wildly. I should have gone for help. Maybe—but no, help was too far away. He knew there was nothing he could have done. And the man had used his dying strength to deliver his message, perhaps even hastening his end in doing so.

David looked at the deathly white, bloodied face. Just an ordinary man, nothing special about him: thin, curly hair; a slightly crooked nose; a square chin. What was he mixed up in that his last desperate wish was to have a certain paper delivered to an unnamed man?

The paper. David gave up trying to loosen the knot, cut the lace and unhooked it, then worked the boot over the heel. A piece of paper was taped to the inside of the sole. He peeled it off, tape and all, and thrust it into his pocket with the brooch and feather.

He pulled the boot back onto the foot. He should do it up properly again so no one would know. At least that was the impression he got—that this whole thing was something secret. Maybe he shouldn't have cut the lace, but that couldn't be helped now. Surely no one would notice—

Suddenly David's head jerked up. Someone was running towards him.

He rehooked the boot as tightly as he could, then pushed the cut end under one of the top hooks and tried to hide it with the knot. That would have to do. He made sure the paper and brooch were safely in his pocket.

The steps were coming closer. David stood up, his knees shaking. "Hello? Someone there? Help!"

The running stopped abruptly. David could faintly make out a figure, a darker shape in the mist.

"Hello. Where are you?"

"Here, by the cliff. There's an injured man here. I think he's dead."

A stocky man solidified out of the mist. As he drew closer David was aware of dark, penetrating eyes beneath what looked like a single black brow.

The man squatted beside the form at David's feet. "How long ago did this happen?"

"I don't know. I was walking along the beach when I heard him call out a few minutes ago. I think he just died. He *is* dead, isn't he?"

"Yes, he's dead. You didn't hear him fall?"

"No. He must have fallen quite a while before I came along."

"Did he say anything to you before he died?"

David was aware that he was being watched

closely. "No." He hoped his hesitation had gone unnoticed. "At least not that I could make out. He called for help. That's how I knew he was here. Then he kept trying to say something. That his leg hurt, something like that."

The man grunted and turned to the corpse again.

"This your coat? You might as well take it. He'll not be wanting it anymore."

David had forgotten the coat, had even been unaware of the heavy mist soaking into his sweater, running down his face.

"I'll look after things here, lad. Why don't you go back to the hotel and get dried out. You know the way all right? Tell Ian, the manager. He'll know what to do."

David nodded. "I'll be as fast as I can."

* * *

At the local police station it seemed the only matter of any consequence was the brewing of a pot of tea, but David was glad of a few minutes to relax. In the excitement back at the hotel he had had no time to consider his situation seriously. After changing into dry clothes he had accompanied the ambulance to the beach and led the attendants to the body. Then, along with the man who had joined him there, he had been whisked off to the police station.

Now the excitement had subsided. With the observation, "You will be needing a hot cup of tea after your experience," the grey-haired sergeant had disappeared. A young constable had offered his guests a bag of mints.

In the hospitable atmosphere David slowly relaxed. The scene at the foot of the cliff was still vivid in his mind and he wondered what he should do. He needed time to think it all out.

He opened his eyes to meet those of the man who had found him at the cliff. The dark eyes beneath the single brow were watching him speculatively. The man smiled a little, a smile that touched his mouth but somehow failed to reach his eyes.

"We're never in a hurry in these parts, lad," he said. "We call it Highland time."

"It suits me anyway," said David. "I'm ready for that cup of tea."

It was worth waiting for too, he decided a few minutes later as he sipped the steaming liquid carefully. For the next few minutes there was satisfied silence in the police station.

It was the man with the eyebrow who finally broached the subject. "Sergeant," he said, "can you tell us who the dead man was?"

"Cairns," replied the policeman. "John Edward Cairns." He reluctantly pushed his empty cup aside and took up a notebook and pencil. "With the firm of Cairns and Ross, Estate Agents in Edinburgh. Does that mean anything to either of you?"

They both shook their heads. The sergeant nodded. "No, I thought not. That's all we know so far, but we're expecting further word from Edinburgh any minute."

"He wasn't staying at the hotel," volunteered Eyebrow, but the sergeant made no comment.

"Now," he continued in an official tone, "if you two gentlemen have any identification..."

He took David's passport first. "*David Mc-Crimmon of Woodstock, Ontario, Canada. Brown hair, blue eyes.* On holiday, Mr. Mc-Crimmon?"

"Yes. I landed in Prestwick last Wednesday and I'll be here until late August."

"And what will you be meaning, precisely, by 'here'?"

"I mean in Scotland, just travelling. Mainly in the Hebrides."

"Have you relatives here then?"

"Some cousins somewhere in Skye. My mother was a war bride from Skye. All her immediate family are in Canada now and we kind of lost touch with the cousins."

"Aye, that happens. And where have you been since Wednesday?"

"I spent the first night in Largs, then I was on Arran for two days. Later I came over to the coast and I've been hiking up this way, staying at bed-and-breakfasts."

"How did you happen to come to the Boar's Head Inn?"

"I was given a ride by a farmer who lives nearby. It was raining and the hotel was handy."

"I see. That was last night? Aye. Now, about this morning. How did you happen to find the victim, Mr. McCrimmon?"

David told him. The policeman nodded thoughtfully.

"You are certain you heard nothing earlier? No sound that might have been a body falling, or a shout maybe?"

"No, nothing at all. I think he must have fallen some time before I came along."

"Aye, it looks like it. Now"—he turned to the other man's documents—"Mr. Brieve, is it?"

"Yes. Adam Brieve. I'm engineer aboard the *Island Phantom*."

"Rory MacLeod's boat? Whatever happened to Willie Murray? He was Rory's engineer for years."

"He had an accident a month or so ago. He'll be in a wheelchair for a long time."

"Aye, of course, I had forgotten. A hit-and-run." The sergeant shook his head. "So you're the new engineer? But Rory's not down this way, is he?"

"No. I've been down to Glasgow to see my sister who's been ill. Rory's not expecting me for another day or two, so I stopped in at the Boar's Head for a bit of angling. I just arrived last night, too late to go out, and then this morning—"

"Tell us about this morning."

"Well, I went down to the river about seven. Tried several spots with no luck. I saw the lad here—Mr. McCrimmon—go by about nine o'clock. Is that right, Mr. McCrimmon?"

"When I went along by the river?" David reflected. "Yes, I guess it was about nine."

"I noticed him go to the shore," Brieve continued, "and turn down the beach. It was a beautiful morning then, but I knew the mist would be coming in soon and in a fog like that a stranger

9

might easily get lost. So I went after him in case he needed help."

David looked up in surprise. It had never occurred to him that *he* might have been in any need of help. After all, he had been at the foot of the cliff, not at the top.

"It's too bad you didn't see Mr. Cairns and go to *his* help," the sergeant said. "How did you know the lad was a stranger?"

"Ian Campbell, the proprietor of the Boar's Head, told me about him last night."

"Right enough. And Mr. Cairns was dead when you got there, was he, Mr. Brieve?"

"Yes, but only just. He was still warm."

The policeman nodded. He indicated to the constable that the teacups should be refilled and was silent while this was being done.

"Indications are that the victim fell over the cliff in the fog and was killed," he finally observed. "Would either of you say there was anything about the body or about the situation to contradict that?"

David was surprised again. "Not me," he said. "Nothing else ever occurred to me."

"Nor you, Mr. Brieve?"

"Well"—the man with the eyebrow hesitated— "I noticed one thing I thought rather odd, Sergeant. The lace on one of his boots was cut."

David's heart skipped a beat. He suddenly realized that Adam Brieve was looking directly at him, not at the policeman. Perhaps now was the time to tell. But no, he wasn't going to say anything yet, not until he had time to reason it out.

"Mr. McCrimmon? Did you notice that?"

10

"No, I didn't pay any attention to his boots." David hoped guilt wasn't apparent in his voice. "He was still alive so I put my coat over him, but I guess I didn't look at his feet."

"Well, it's odd, as you say, Mr. Brieve, but it's hard to say what it might mean. When we know a little more about the man we'll be further ahead." He closed his notebook and returned to his teacup. "I'm afraid we'll have to ask both of you to stay nearby for a while. By tomorrow we should know if there's to be an inquest. Under the circumstances it isn't likely, but you never know what an investigation might turn up. I hope that will not inconvenience you?"

He didn't wait for an answer. "Perhaps you could make arrangements for one more night at the Boar's Head. Our car will take you back there if you like."

Looking outside, David saw that the mist had vanished and the brooding hills were beckoning. "Thanks all the same," he said, "but I'll walk."

Leaving the police station, he headed out of town. He followed a cart track for a while, then turned off over the moors and ascended gradually to the crest of a long hill. Rabbits darted away at his approach. Sheep looked at him briefly, then ignored him. Otherwise the world was silent and still save when the heather moved at the whim of a wayward breeze.

The crest was farther off than he had anticipated, but he reached it eventually and paused to look around. A vista of undulating hills lay on all sides with the sea to the west, island-flecked, bright in the sun.

The heather was deep and comfortable. David sat down and with quickening pulse took out the paper he had removed from the dying man's boot. It was a map, roughly drawn but unmistakable. Even without the inked markings he would have recognized the Outer Hebrides—Lewis, Harris, the Uists, Barra—from his familiarity with the tourist map. But this map also included a string of tiny islands to the west of the Long Island.

Very small, probably uninhabited, David decided. There were many such islands throughout the Hebridean area, of too little importance to appear on a tourist map. But one of them, slightly to the west and south of the rest, was marked with an asterisk, its name underlined: *Sgeir Dubh.*

He knew that *dubh* meant black. Black something, thought David. But what did *sgeir* mean? Headland, was that it? Promontory? Rock? Something like that. Yes, of course, a sea rock. Black Rock Island.

Now what was so important about Black Rock Island that a man would carry a map stressing its location hidden in the sole of his boot?

The boot, of course, was the crux of the whole affair. Perhaps if it wasn't for that... David slowly refolded the map, then noticed something else, a few words written after it had been folded once: *We are right about X. You know what to do.*

There was nothing else anywhere on the map. He returned it to his pocket and lay back in the heather, his hands clasped behind his head. A man, his body shattered by a fall, his life slipping away, concerned only about a paper . . .

But perhaps he hadn't realized the seriousness of his situation. Perhaps he hadn't known he was dying. No, that wouldn't wash, David decided. When I suggested going for help he protested so strongly. He *had* known. And his main concern had been that the paper be delivered to a certain unnamed person, to be contacted through a brooch bearing a gull's feather. Why the mysterious precautions?

David reran the morning's events through his mind. The police had identified the dead man as an estate agent. As such he had every right to be interested in islands and to be anxious to pass information on to a colleague. Perhaps he had a prospective buyer for Black Rock Island. Perhaps it was a big deal involving millions and others wanted to block the deal or to get their share. But why a map in a boot?

That darn boot! If there's a simple explanation for that, David thought, it beats me.

He took the brooch from his pocket and examined it—a cheap chrome-plated lapel pin with a gull's feather stuck between the paws of the rearing lion. It told him nothing. Frowning, he pinned the brooch and map together, returned them to his pocket, stood up and began to walk on.

Was he going to go through with the dying man's request? That was what he had to decide. Or should he get out from under by telling the police the whole story?

That, really, was the sensible course. He

couldn't have told the police during the recent interview, not with Adam Brieve there listening— that would have been betraying a trust. But there was no reason why he couldn't go back now.

Except that he had given his word to a dying man. Could he go back on that?

David thought of the moment during the interview when Adam had mentioned the cut boot lace. If there were an inquest and that came up he'd have to tell the truth before an entire court-room. And that, surely, was the last thing the dead man would have wanted.

Well, he decided, if there's to be an inquest I'll tell the police everything beforehand. If not, I'll go through with it.

After all, it was a simple thing he had been asked to do. And it was probably the only way he would discover the significance of the curious map.

2

It was dusk when David finally returned to the hotel, tired and hungry after a day on the moors. He hung his jacket on the rack in the dining room and in a few minutes was making short work of a big meal.

Ten minutes later Adam Brieve came in. He hung his jacket carefully beside David's and started towards an empty table. Then he suddenly glanced at his watch, frowned and abruptly turned and went out.

Must have remembered something, David guessed.

Adam returned later as David was starting his dessert. He paused at the coat rack again. Then, as he turned, his eye caught David's and he nodded. When David indicated the empty chair across from him Adam took it.

"I was looking for you earlier," he said. "Did you have a good day?"

David nodded. "Great. I enjoy walking and I did plenty of that. I had no idea how late it was even though I was getting hungry."

"Did you know the police were looking for you maybe an hour ago?"

"Oh-oh." David looked up anxiously. "Not another delay, I hope?"

"No. Just the opposite, in fact. We can leave whenever we like, it seems, just as long as they know where they can get in touch with us."

"Darn!" David frowned in annoyance. "That's a real nuisance. I don't know *where* I'll be. I want to be free to come and go as I please—that's to be half the fun of this holiday. No timetables. No clocks."

"Then you have no immediate plans?"

"No. Well, I figured on taking the noon boat to Tobermory on Friday. After that, wherever the whim takes me."

"The noon boat from Oban? Since you're travelling free of timetables could you make it the morning boat? I'll be taking that one myself and I could maybe show you some of the points of interest."

"That would have been good," said David regretfully, "but I, uh, prefer the noon boat." So much for freedom of movement, he thought.

But Adam apparently noticed no contradiction. "Oh, well, too bad. But you will be here among the Isles for the next week, won't you? The police shouldn't be wanting you after that."

"Oh, yes. I'll be somewhere in the Hebrides all month, maybe all summer. But I suppose the police will want more than somewhere in the Hebrides for an address."

"Yes, no doubt. But I think perhaps I can help you. As you know, I'm engineer aboard a boat that sails among the Western Isles. The *Island Phantom* she's called, though she's known as the *Bochan* by most people. Rory MacLeod sails her and no one knows the Isles better than Rory. You'll never see the Islands, nor hear about them, better than you would on Rory's boat."

"You mean he takes passengers?"

"Well, now, I wouldn't say that," said Adam cautiously. "He doesn't sell tickets and would turn down most tourists if they should apply for passage. It has to be someone special or he'll not be interested."

David looked at Adam hopefully. "Do you think I might qualify as someone special?"

"Yes, I do. Besides the circumstances—the police and all—there's your name. It's a well-known one in the Isles. The McCrimmons were famous bagpipe players in the old days. And there's your love of the Hebrides. As Rory would say, you've heard the call of the Isles—or am I wrong?"

As Adam spoke David recalled his first view of the Hebrides, spread out in mystic splendour across the face of the sea, their strange shapes and the purple-dyed hills bringing a lump to his throat, a plucking at his heart and a spring to his step.

"The call of the Isles. Yes, I guess that just about says it all. You think that's enough to get me an invitation aboard?"

"I think so. With a word from me, of course, just to add some weight. What do you think?"

"Well," David hesitated, "there's just one thing. I'm travelling on a shoestring, so to speak. I have to find the cheapest route wherever I go. I shouldn't have stayed in this hotel at all, let alone two nights. Do you think I might be allowed to work my passage?"

"It wouldn't be a bad idea to offer, though I'm sure you wouldn't be working very hard. The *Bochan* will be in Tobermory all day Friday, so you won't miss her if you take the noon boat. I'll explain the circumstances to Rory. This way the police will have a line on you and you won't be wasting time staying in one place."

"Right. That's a great idea. Thanks very much."

"No bother," Adam said. "I'll see you in Tobermory on Friday."

A few minutes later David left the room, taking his jacket from the rack on the way out. He patted the pocket that held the map and brooch and his heart skipped a beat. The pocket was empty.

For a moment he looked around anxiously. Had they fallen? Then he relaxed and sighed with relief. Wrong side—they were in the other one. Funny. He could have sworn he'd left them both in the right-hand pocket.

* * *

The brooch and feather remained in David's pocket—a fact he frequently verified—until the *Skerryvore* slipped her moorings at noon on Friday and passed out into the Sound. As the boat cast off he pinned the brooch to his jacket. One thing for sure, he thought wryly, his contact would have no problem identifying him. There was a distinct lack of gull's feathers adorning his fellow passengers.

But no one took the slightest notice of it—not even Adam Brieve.

David looked up in surprise as the squat figure of the engineer appeared beside him. "I thought you were planning on taking the morning boat," he said.

"I was, but I missed it." Adam shrugged carelessly. "No bother. The *Island Phantom* won't be leaving until the morning. Do you still want to join me on board?"

"Oh, yes. I'm looking forward to it. I'm glad you're here—I was afraid I might miss you in Tobermory and lose out on the deal. Besides, you volunteered to act as my guide on the way up the Sound, remember?"

"Right enough, so I did." Adam turned to watch Oban harbour slipping slowly astern. He waved his arm to encompass the surrounding countryside. "They call this area the District of Lorne."

"I know," nodded David. "Once it was dominated by the MacDougalls, but they backed the wrong side in the wars of independence and lost it. Now, of course, it's Campbell country."

"Oh, uh, yes." Adam was somewhat taken aback. "Perhaps you won't be needing a guide after all."

He was quite right. It was David who gave Adam a lesson in history, recounting the stories of Duart and Ardtornish Castles and the Lady's Rock. It wasn't long before Adam threw up his hands in surrender.

"Lad," he said, "you know more about this area than many of the locals. I can see you'll get along fine with Rory on the *Bochan*." He clapped David on the shoulder. "I'm away below now to have a crack with the engineer, but don't forget, I'll see you in Tobermory."

David was relieved to see him go. He didn't want Adam hanging around when someone recognized the feather on his jacket and approached him for the map. He found a deck chair on the port side and sat down, put his feet on the lower rail and happily watched sun and shadow play tag across the lovely hills of Mull.

He was aroused a few minutes later when a man paused at his side. He was a big man dressed in tweeds, solidly built, with iron-grey hair and matching moustache, and with a short pipe clenched between his teeth.

The man removed the pipe and indicated the chair beside David. "Is this seat taken?"

"No," said David, faintly surprised for there were plenty of empty chairs.

"Good." The man sat down and made himself comfortable. "A beautiful, clear day to make the trip."

"Yes," nodded David. "Thank goodness. It's my first time."

"Is it now?" The man was looking at him with interest. "Are you going all the way around?"

"Around Mull, you mean? No, not this time. Just to Tobermory."

"That's too bad. I think the last leg of the trip across the south of Mull and back to Oban is the best part. You can see the Islands of the Sea as well as Islay and Jura, and away beyond Oban to the peaks of Cruachan. That is, if you're lucky and the weather co-operates." He leaned forward and tapped the bowl of his pipe on the rail. Then he looked at David.

"I'm Ramshaw," he said.

"How do you do, Mr. Ramshaw. My name's David McCrimmon."

"Is it?" The man was looking at him keenly. "I thought maybe it was Johnny Cairns."

For a fraction of a second the significance of the name escaped David. Then abruptly he remembered. John Edward Cairns. The dead man.

"Ah. You evidently know the name." Ramshaw sat back, satisfied.

David bit his lip. His start at the name had given him away. No use denying that it was familiar to him.

The man was speaking again. "I've been in something of a quandary ever since leaving Oban. It looked as if either John Cairns was a much younger man than I had reason to believe, or there were actually two people wearing"—he indicated David's brooch and feather—"a rampant lion and gull's feather. Incredible, but I looked anyway. I assure you there is no one else so decorated on board. Therefore, either John Cairns can disguise himself to look half his age or he has an accomplice."

He began to press some fresh tobacco into his pipe with a blunt thumb. He looked at David. "I believe you have a message for me."

David hesitated, then nodded. "I guess I have. Somehow I didn't expect to meet you so soon. I don't remember the exact words, but I got the idea we would meet in Tobermory—probably on the dock."

"Oh, yes, that's maybe how he saw it. In fact, that's how it would have happened except that I had to go to the mainland yesterday and it was convenient for me to return by this boat. Works out well, in fact—it will give us more time to get acquainted. Tell me, how do you explain someone of your years doing Cairns' work for him?"

"Well, Mr. Cairns didn't have much choice." David told Ramshaw how he had acquired the message.

Ramshaw said nothing for a moment. He took his time applying a match to his pipe and puffing it into life. David found it impossible to read any thoughts behind the man's expression.

"So," he observed at last, "John Edward Cairns is dead. But his work didn't die with him, thanks to you. You did very well. Why didn't you just go to the police?"

"I thought about it," admitted David. "But I made a promise to Cairns and he died believing I was going to do as he asked. It was very important to him." He hesitated, then remembered something else. "I might still have to go to the police, you know. There could be an inquest."

But Ramshaw shook his head. "I can set your mind at rest on that point. There will be no public enquiry. As soon as they find out who he was I'm sure the police will turn the whole matter over to MI5."

"MI5?" David's pulse quickened. "That's Military Intelligence, isn't it? You mean he was a spy?"

Ramshaw nodded. "That's right, an intelligence agent. A spy if you like. Didn't that occur to you before?"

"No, not really. You know, guys like David McCrimmon from Woodstock, Ontario, don't get mixed up in espionage. Not in real life. So you must be a spy too."

"Well, not in the sense that Cairns was. None of that cloak-and-dagger stuff for me. I doubt that Cairns was even his real name, and I don't know what he looked like. Hence all this." He indicated the feather again. "With me it's usually just a desk job.

"We owe you a debt of gratitude for all you've done, McCrimmon. I know you must be very curious, but you'll appreciate that I can't explain everything to you—though maybe I can tell you a bit more after I see whatever message Cairns had for me."

"It's a map. I looked at it," David admitted, "to see what I was getting into."

"Naturally. You're only human. I wouldn't have believed you if you'd denied it." Ramshaw paused expectantly.

David reached into his pocket, then looked around quickly. No one was paying any attention and there was no sign of Adam.

Ramshaw caught the action and his eyebrows rose questioningly.

"The man who came along just after I found Cairns is here on the *Skerryvore* and sometimes I think he's just a bit suspicious of me. He noticed the cut boot lace and he seems to turn up every so often, as if he's keeping an eye on me."

"Adam Brieve, you said his name was? I know him. Engineer on the *Island Phantom*. Well, I don't think I would worry about him too much— after all, what meaning can one possibly read into a cut boot lace? Still, you're quite right to keep your eyes open. No use giving him anything else to wonder about. If he sees us together, we just fell into conversation and I'm telling you a bit about the Islands."

David grinned. "Adam tried that and I ended up telling him."

"Oh, so that's the way of it? All right, you're telling me. Anyway, he's nowhere in sight so you can give me the message."

Ramshaw took the map and spread it out on his knee. David saw him frown and shake his head ever so slightly. Then he refolded it, noting as he did so the written message.

"Not what you expected?" ventured David.

"It *is* what I expected," said Ramshaw, "but not what I hoped for." He slipped the map into his pocket. "Look, David, let's go below for a cup of tea. I've got to think this over for a few minutes."

They found their way to the lounge and sat at a corner table away from anyone else. After a few silent minutes Ramshaw looked at David. "Tell me about yourself, lad."

"Well, there's not much to tell. My great-grandparents emigrated to Canada from Skye. My dad came over here in the Second World War

—he was in the Navy—and visited Skye. It was his first visit to his ancestral home and he fell in love with it. And with a Skye girl too. She came to Canada after the war and married Dad and eventually I came along. You might say I was brought up on a diet of the Hebrides in general and Skye in particular. I've always dreamed about coming over and now I'm here."

"And how does it measure up? Apart from this Cairns business, of course."

"It's everything I expected. Actually, it's going to get better than I ever hoped."

"Why do you say that?"

"It's thanks to Adam Brieve. He's going to arrange a trip for me aboard the *Island Phantom*."

"Adam Brieve again, eh?" Ramshaw was thoughtful for a moment, then roused himself. "Well, I'm glad that's been arranged. It means you've got some reward for what you've done. And you'll certainly find out more about the Hebrides from Rory MacLeod than you would from any number of guidebooks or conducted tours. You'll like Rory—not to mention his niece Sandy. It's an interesting development. And frustrating."

"Frustrating?" David looked at him curiously. "Why frustrating?"

"It's this way," said Ramshaw. "This Cairns business should be all over as far as you're concerned. I have no right to ask you to do any more than you've already done, but it's a sore temptation." He paused. "If you're going to be on the *Bochan* there's one more thing you could do for me."

David grinned. "You've succeeded in making

me curious anyway. Maybe if you could tell me what you have in mind . . . "

"I've just been wondering how much I should tell you." Ramshaw was silent for a moment, turning things over in his mind. "First, I must impress upon you the importance of silence. This isn't a matter to fool around with. We have one victim already—"

"Victim!" Suddenly David sat up straight. "You mean that Cairns was murdered?"

"No, no, David, I'm not saying that. Mind you, I'm not denying it. Cairns was a man who flirted with danger every day of his life. Someone who had nothing to do with this matter may have simply caught up with him. I'm just saying that we can't be too careful. That's why I'm going to tell you only a part of it—the less you know the better. Already you must be eager to tell others of your experience, but right now you mustn't say a word to anyone. Two weeks from now all right, say what you like. But right now, no."

"You mean it will be all over in two weeks?"

"Yes, I'd say so. One way or another." He was looking at David keenly. "You can end your involvement right now or you can do one more thing. Nothing dangerous or spectacular—plenty of espionage is plain dull work, you know. Not all of it is the cloak-and-dagger stuff you read about." He paused again, then said abruptly, "Have you heard anything about submarines being reported in the Hebridean area?"

"Submarines? Ye-es, I think someone at the Boar's Head did mention something—made a joke of it. But that's all."

Ramshaw nodded. "Yes. Well, I expect you'll hear more in the next few days. You see, there have been several reported sightings where no submarines should be." He opened the map. "We consider two of the reports reliable. A lighthouse keeper out in the Flannans saw one on the surface between two fog banks. All black, no markings whatever. The other was in the North Minch, east of the Butt. She was spotted by the crew of a fishery inspection ship—showed up on the radar at night and they turned the light on her, thinking she was a trawler, and saw her submerging. Same description as the other sighting." Ramshaw chuckled. "Other reports put submarines in various places—a little imagination or a few too many in the pub and submarines begin to show up all over. But we don't take any of the reports too seriously except those two."

"But whose submarines could they be? What would they be doing in this area?"

Ramshaw shook his head. "The less you know the easier it will be to keep quiet. You can take my word for it that there *has* been a submarine, and more than that, that it has a secret base somewhere in the Islands."

"A base?" David shook his head. "I didn't hear any rumours about that. Is that why that island was marked on the map? Sgeir Dubh?"

Ramshaw nodded. "We had the first hint of something illegal going on from a man you might call a freelance spy—one of those people who make a living ferreting out information and peddling it to the highest bidder. We put Cairns onto it. Indications were that there is a sub in this area, that she has a base from which she operates and that the head of the whole operation is a man who lives somewhere in the Hebrides. Our job has been to locate the base and to identify the head man, referred to rather unimaginatively as X. That's what this map and the note are all about.

"We have a pretty good suspicion as to the identity of X, and apparently Cairns found some information to back this up. Also, it looks as if he believed the island being used as a base is the one marked on the map. Sgeir Dubh." Ramshaw frowned and shook his head. "In this case I very much fear he has been misled, since further information indicates a base in another area entirely." He tapped his pipe in the ashtray. "I'm sorry I can't be more explicit, but I'll explain why I've told you as much as I have. No one knows the Islands better than Rory MacLeod. If there's an island anywhere in the Hebrides that would be particularly suitable as a submarine base, Rory would know it."

"So why not ask him?"

"Because our official position is that the sighted submarines were Royal Navy on legitimate manoeuvres. Under those circumstances I can't approach Rory without taking him into our confidence. It's not that we don't trust him. The simple truth is that the fewer people who know, the better—and safer—for all. On the other hand there would be nothing suspicious in your asking him."

David nodded slowly. "I see what you mean. Rory will have heard the rumour about the sub.

But have there been any rumours about a base?"

Ramshaw shook his head. "Not yet." He smiled. "You will have to start one. I suggest you tell Rory you heard a rumour that an unknown submarine has a base in the Hebrides and ask him if that would be possible—and what island *he* would pick as the most suitable."

David nodded again. "Sounds easy enough. Is that all you want me to do?"

"That's all." Ramshaw took a card from his pocket. "Rory's home port is Calluig, a village on the west coast of Lewis. My home"—he indicated the card—"is Ramshaw Castle, between Calluig and Stornoway."

"Ramshaw Castle? A *real* castle?"

Ramshaw nodded, his eyes twinkling. "A real castle. Originally belonging to the Morrisons of Ramshaw, but they died out some time ago and the castle was unattended until my father bought it and became the Laird of Ramshaw—although his name, like mine, was actually Fletcher. My man there, Aulay MacLure, will be glad to give you all the history of the castle and its original owners, as well as a guided tour if you're interested."

"That sounds great. I guess I am being well rewarded for carrying out a dying man's request: a trip on the *Island Phantom* and a visit to a castle I might never have heard of otherwise."

It had all been very lucky, he mused. But there was another thought lurking in the back of his mind. The thought that John Edward Cairns' accident might not have been an accident at all.

3

By the time the *Skerryvore* sailed into Tobermory Bay the mist had descended, blotting out
the far shore and lying like a blanket across the
mirror-calm surface. The village houses climbed
the steep flanks of the hill into oblivion and
ghostly wraiths swirled about the towers of the
Western Isles Hotel.

Ramshaw had joined David at the rail. "It's
maybe a good thing you're not going any farther
today after all. You'd not see much in this mist.
We do have fine weather, you know, occasionally.
With luck the sun will be shining when you sail
on the *Bochan*. You have my card?"

David nodded.

"Good. Call me when you reach Calluig and
I'll send a car for you. If Rory and his niece
would like to come along for a visit too, they're
more than welcome. Meantime"—Ramshaw drew
the gull's feather and brooch from his pocket,
pinned the brooch to his own lapel and stuck the
feather into David's buttonhole—"a souvenir and
a seal to our bargain."

Before David could answer, Adam Brieve shouldered through the crowd. "Ah, there you are." He saw Ramshaw and hesitated.

"Adam Brieve, isn't it?" Ramshaw thrust out his hand. "How are you? Still working for Rory, I hear."

"Yes, that's right, as engineer on the *Bochan*. She's out there somewhere." He waved in the direction of the mist-shrouded harbour, then looked from one to the other.

"Have you two met, then?"

"Yes, we've met," said David, "and I've been invited out to Ramshaw Castle when we get to Calluig."

"Have you now?" exclaimed Adam. "Well, that's just fine." He turned towards the bay as the *Skerryvore* eased alongside the jetty. "You can see the *Island Phantom* now, lad." He pointed to where an indistinct shape had materialized, riding at anchor in the bay. "They should be sending a boat over for me soon, but I have to go up to the hotel to meet a friend. Perhaps you wouldn't mind waiting on the dock until the boat arrives, David, to tell whoever it is—Seumas, or maybe Andra—that I'll not be back for two hours. Then you could look around the town and we could meet on the dock again at, say, five o'clock. Is that all right?"

"Okay, five o'clock, then. But how will I know Seumas or Andra?"

"You can't mistake either one," laughed Ramshaw. "They're both big braw men with black hair and gigantic hooked beaks, and if they say more than two words they're not Seumas or Andra."

"You know them, sir," grinned Adam. He clapped David on the shoulder. "There's the gangway down. I'll see you on the dock at five o'clock."

David hoisted his knapsack to his shoulders and followed Adam and the Laird. Adam disappeared quickly, but Ramshaw remained near David as the throng disembarked. As they walked down the gangway one man standing near the end of it caught David's attention. He was an odd little man in a bowler hat and dark suit. His eyes were badly crossed. He was undoubtedly watching the retreating passengers with one eye, but the other might have been trying to pierce the mist above the town.

The man stepped forward and seemed about to speak to David. Then he saw Ramshaw. "Oh, Ramshaw . . . How are you?"

"Hello, Professor. I'm just fine, thanks. How are you yourself?"

"I had a bit of a fall on the rocks at St. Kilda, but otherwise I'm very well."

"St. Kilda! Crawling over those steep cliffs looking for birds' eggs, I suppose. Professor, you're lucky you weren't killed long ago." Ramshaw shook his head in mock despair. "By the way, I'd like you to meet a friend of mine. This is David McCrimmon from Canada, who has just arrived to visit the Isles. David, this is Professor Sulsted, one of the greatest living authorities on sea birds."

"How do you do." David found the intensity of the gaze from one of the eyes rather disconcerting. "I'm sure sea birds must be an interesting study."

"Ha!" said the little man. Both eyes managed to converge momentarily. "You like birds, do you?"

"Oh, uh, yes, of course. But I'm afraid I don't really know much about them—I live a long way from the ocean. They're all just gulls to me."

The little man shook his head sorrowfully. "Gulls!" he sighed. He reached forward and jabbed a finger at the feather still stuck in David's buttonhole. "You don't even know the difference between a herring gull and a guillemot, do you?"

"'Fraid not," admitted David, feeling a bit guilty.

"Come, come, Professor," said Ramshaw. "We can't all be bird fanciers, you know. To each his own. You experts think we should all share your interests. I wouldn't know a guillemot if I tripped over one myself."

"Oh, well." The little man spread his hands in resignation. "We will forget the birds. I hope you enjoy your stay with us, young man."

"He will," said Ramshaw. He turned to David. "I'm away then, lad. I'll be looking forward to your visit."

He walked away rapidly, leaving David to watch the activities as the *Skerryvore* prepared to slip her lines. It was some moments before he was aware that the professor was still there, and that at least one eye appeared to be watching him curiously. David felt a little uncomfortable.

"You mentioned St. Kilda," he said, to make conversation. "I'd like to go out there before I go home."

"Why? Unless you're a climber I wouldn't advise it," Sulsted replied. "There's nothing there but birds and cliffs. Do you climb?"

"No," admitted David. "We don't have any cliffs around home, but I do enjoy beautiful scenery."

"Well, you'll see plenty of that." When David said nothing more the little man seemed to suddenly lose interest in him. Without another word he turned and walked away.

David watched him go, half amused, half puzzled, then forgot him as the propeller of the *Skerryvore* broke into life and churned the water into a froth. The ship eased away from the dock, slid easily over the calm water, blended into the mists and disappeared.

David unshouldered his knapsack and sat down on a bollard. All at once he was aware of the silence, a silence pressed down by the mists, pierced now and then by the harsh cry of a gull.

Suddenly that silence was broken by the *putt-putt* of a small outboard somewhere in the bay.

David peered into the mists and saw a small shape detach itself from the grey shadow that was the *Island Phantom.* A boat approached, splitting the glass-smooth water into long, rolling furrows. But it was obviously not one of Ramshaw's "braw men" at the tiller.

The engine cut off and the boat glided out of sight below the dock. After a moment the boat's operator climbed up the ladder and stepped nimbly onto the jetty. Instead of the black hair and gigantic beak Ramshaw had described there were reddish-brown waves and a small nose sprinkled with freckles. And the mouth, David suspected, would produce a dimple at a moment's notice.

The girl glanced briefly at David, turned toward town, looked at her watch, then turned back to him again, frankly curious.

"Hi," said David tentatively.

"Hello." Her eyes went to his knapsack. "If you're waiting for a bus there aren't all that many that come along the jetty." David's suspicions about the dimple were confirmed.

"Actually," he said, "I think I've been waiting for you. Have you come for Adam Brieve?"

"Yes." Her eyebrows rose questioningly.

"He asked me to tell you that he won't be back until five o'clock. Are you Seumas or Andra?"

She laughed and it was a nice sound. "I'm Sandy," she said. "Who are you? A friend of Adam's?"

"I'm David McCrimmon. I met Adam a couple of days ago at a hotel south of Oban—we were both hauled into the police station at the same time. And then we met again on the *Skerry-vore—*"

"Wait a minute." She stood there frowning. "You met him in a hotel? Where was that?"

"Nowhere. I mean, the hotel isn't in any town. It's just by itself out in the country. The Boar's Head."

"Oh, aye. I know it. But what was Adam doing there? I mean—" She hesitated.

"I think he said he had some extra time before your ship was due to sail so he stopped by for some fishing," said David.

"Fishing? Adam?" She sounded incredulous. "And what was that about the police?"

"Well," he continued, "it was foggy—like today, only worse—and raining, and a man fell over the cliff. I happened to find him and Adam came along just after."

"Oh dear! Was the man badly hurt?"

"I'm afraid so. He died just after I found him, so we had to go to the police station to give our statements."

"I'm sorry," she said. "It must have been awful. Will there be an inquest, do you think?"

"There might be," nodded David. "And that's really why I'm here. You see, I'm in Scotland on holiday and I wanted to be free to come and go as I please, anywhere in the Hebridean area. Trouble is, the police said they have to have an address where they can get in touch with me in case of an inquest. That's when Adam had a brainwave."

"Adam did?" Her tone suggested that might be a rare occurrence.

"Yes. He suggested that I could sail on the *Island Phantom* with him. That way the police could reach us both and at the same time I could see something of the Hebrides. More of the Hebrides, in fact, than in any other way."

"Adam suggested that?" She shook her head, puzzled. "The man's full of surprises."

David looked at her anxiously. "I hope he didn't speak out of turn," he said. "I'd expect to work my way, of course—"

"Oh, no. I'm sorry. Of course you're welcome to come aboard. Uncle Rory—that's Rory MacLeod, the skipper—will be pleased to have you if you're interested in the Isles. Did you say you're a McCrimmon? Well, then, you're a Hebridean wherever you come from. Are you an American?"

"No, I'm from Canada. Woodstock, Ontario. You've heard of it, no doubt."

"Woodstock?" She shook her head. "I don't think so. Should I have?"

"Oh, yes. We're famous for having a statue to our local heroine."

"But lots of places have statues like that."

"But to a cow?"

"A *cow!* Your local heroine is a cow? You're joking."

"Not at all. A world-champion butterfat-producing cow. Never was another like her. And our city hall is supposed to be a replica of the one in Woodstock, England. Maybe I'll have a chance to check that out before I go home."

"It sounds like a quaint place." She sounded a little doubtful.

David laughed. "It's home anyway. But my people came from Skye and they've told me so much about the Hebrides that I've dreamed almost all my life of coming here and exploring. And," he added, "not only am I going to sail on your boat, but I have an invitation to visit a genuine castle and dine with the Laird."

"Oh? You do work fast. What castle would that be?"

"Ramshaw Castle. Do you know it?"

"Oh, yes, I know it, of course. And the Laird. But he never invited *me* to his castle."

"Well, you're invited now," David assured her. "He told me to bring you and your uncle along."

"Did he? Well that was decent of him," said Sandy, mollified. "There are lots of odd tales about that building. Maybe we'll have a chance to explore." She glanced at her watch. "Look, if Adam's not going to be back before five why don't we go out to the *Phantom* now? We can send Seumas back for Adam and you can tell me how you managed to get an invitation to Ramshaw Castle."

Sandy introduced David to the *Island Phantom* with pride and affection in her voice. The *Phantom* had been a trawler originally, or such had been the intention of the builder when she was christened. But the Navy had requisitioned her before a fish was ever tossed into her hold. With modifications, armament and a reserve officer by the name of Rory MacLeod in command she had slogged her way through the war as a hard-working but unspectacular coastal convoy escort.

After the end of hostilities Rory had rescued the *Phantom* from the wreckers, added *Island* to her name and sailed her to the Hebrides. Now she was a familiar sight among the Western Isles. The depth-charge rails were long gone, as was the gun platform, but the open navy-style bridge remained. There Rory conned his little ship, with only the worst the Atlantic could throw at him occasionally driving him to the shelter of the wheelhouse under the bridge. As Sandy and David clambered onto the deck the skipper came to meet them.

"I've brought you a passenger, Uncle Rory," Sandy said, "though you will have to thank Adam for his being here. This is David McCrimmon from Canada. David, this is my Uncle Rory."

There was a rugged, direct quality about the man that appealed at once to David. It was in the deeply-etched lines of his face, the prominent nose, the line of mouth and chin, and most particularly in the deep-set eyes that were, he thought, very like Sandy's.

"Welcome to the Isles, Mr. McCrimmon, and to the *Phantom*. This is indeed a pleasure, though I'm afraid it's a poor welcome for a McCrimmon without the pipes playing. You'll not be a piper yourself, I suppose? No. Oh, well. And it was Adam who brought you to us?"

"Yes." David told his story briefly. "I hope he wasn't too presumptuous when he invited me aboard. He thought maybe if I travelled with you—"

"Yes, yes. *Seadh gu dearbh.* Indeed, you are welcome. I love to show visitors the wonders of God and the glories of the Hebrides. We'll find a bunk for you down in the crew's quarters. Meantime, come with us for a bit of refreshment. We have another guest who will be pleased to meet you before he leaves."

The other guest was seated at a table in the tiny cabin that had once served as a wardroom.

He wore a deerstalker's hat askew on his head and an enormous moustache that extended from his craggy beak almost to the end of his chin.

"Hector, we have a passenger who has come all the way from Canada to see the Isles. David McCrimmon, this is Hector MacNeill."

"*Fàilte do 'n dùthaich,*" roared the man from somewhere behind the moustache. Then he hesitated. "Have you the Gaelic, Mr. McCrimmon?"

"Of course not, Hector," interjected Rory. "They don't have the Gaelic in Canada."

"Well, maybe a few do," qualified David, "but no one that I know. And call me David, please."

"Och, well," said Hector, "maybe you'll join us in a dram for the occasion. Where's the bottle, Sandy?"

"A dram?" David was mystified.

"A shot of whiskey," whispered Sandy. "But I'd advise against it. It's pretty strong stuff." More loudly she said to Hector, "You know fine where the bottle is."

"Will you listen to that now," Hector appealed to David. "Is that any way to talk to an old man? I'll have to hunt for it myself."

The hunt didn't take long as Hector merely opened a cupboard and withdrew a bottle. He held it up to the light and sighed dreamily. "Ah, a beautiful bottle. How many fingers will you be having, lad?"

"Fingers? Oh, no thanks. I think I'll stick to tea."

Hector almost dropped the bottle, but not quite. He gaped at David.

"Rory! Will you look at that now! He won't

take a drink. A McCrimmon and he won't have a dram. Whatever next!" He looked around helplessly at the others, then sighed deeply and shook his head. "Och, well, all the more for the rest of us. You'll join us in a toast anyway, David? Will you be getting me some glasses, Sandy, or must I find them too?"

Sandy obliged by setting four glasses on the table.

Hector dashed the merest splash of liquid into two glasses, which he pushed towards Sandy and David, poured a more generous portion for Rory, then doubled that for himself. Once again he held the bottle up to the light.

"Ah, well," he murmured, "it's maybe just as well David doesn't drink." Then he held the glass aloft. "*Slàinte Mhath!*" he roared.

David looked doubtful. "What's that mean?" he asked.

"Oh, you know. It means good health," said Sandy. "Like *skoal,* or cheers."

"Oh, I get it. Back home they'd say 'Mud in your eye' or 'Bottoms up.'"

Hector released a bellow and slapped the table so that the glasses leapt in the air. "Bottoms up!" he cried and drained his glass at a gulp. The others followed suit more slowly.

"Now, David, tell us how you come to be aboard this good ship."

Once again David told his story. Hector listened and nodded and now and then replenished his glass, each time noting ruefully the new level of liquid in the bottle.

"Well," he observed, "the man who fell over

the cliff has brought you good luck indeed. Otherwise you would not be seeing the Isles from the deck of the *Bochan* and there's no better way to see them. As the Good Book says, 'All things work together for good.' Is that not right, Rory?"

"Aye, as long as you remember the condition, Hector—'to those who love God.' You must not forget that part of it."

"Right enough. If you say so, Rory. He's an elder in the Free Kirk and knows his Bible," he explained to David. "And when the police no longer need to know where you are you can come to visit me. You'll maybe not see as much of the Islands with me, but you'll see them a deal faster."

"Faster? How's that?"

"Hector has the fastest boat in the Western Isles," laughed Sandy. "He needs it to keep ahead of the revenue men. They take a dim view of his private distillery." Then she added, "Would anyone like some scones?"

David grinned his answer. He was going to enjoy being on the *Phantom,* and especially being with Sandy. All in all, the immediate future looked most promising.

4

The *Island Phantom* had cast off and left Tobermory Bay very early the following morning. Now it rounded the north shore of Mull into a wonderland of lonely islands far-flung across the Hebridean Sea.

David stood on the open bridge, a pair of binoculars to his eyes. His delight with the beauty of it all caught his breath. He could feel the lure of those far-distant hills meeting the sky, the restless surge of the sea, the lonely cry of the wheeling seagulls, the fresh breeze whipping back over the forecastle and plucking at his hair. He remembered Adam's mention of the 'call of the Isles' and he knew this was it. The Western Isles were calling and he was answering.

He lowered his glasses and looked at his two companions, Sandy at the wheel and Rory leaning against the binnacle.

"It's beautiful," he said simply.

Rory nodded, pleased. "Aye, it is," he said. "You're fortunate, lad. It's not always like this. Mists, rain—but we can see clearly today." He pointed ahead with the stem of his pipe. "Yonder island is Coll. We're heading for North Uist right now. After that we may turn southward to give you a glimpse of Staffa and the Holy Isle while the weather holds. But perhaps those names mean nothing to you?"

"Yes, they do. I know them. Staffa is where Fingal's Cave is. And the Holy Isle is Iona, where St. Columba landed with the gospel and where kings of Scotland, Ireland and Norway are buried. Right?"

"Aye, that's right. I'm sorry it will be only a glimpse this time, but there will be others. Plenty of tours go to Iona anyway, from Oban or Mull. But first"—he turned and pointed northward—"you will have a grand view to starboard when we sail beyond Ardnamurchan Point. Sandy, let me take the wheel. Ask Tonal to bring us up some lunch. Then you can point out to David the land of his ancestors."

"Skye?" David was surprised. "You can see Skye from here?"

"You will be able to soon."

After Tonal brought their food they watched with teacups in hand as Ardnamurchan lighthouse slipped gradually astern. Then Sandy's hand touched David's arm and she pointed north.

"See those hills, the farthest, the ones that look like the teeth of a saw? Those are the Cuillin Hills."

"So that's Skye I've heard so much about. I think I'm beginning to understand already why Skye people are *always* Skye people."

She nodded, as pleased as Rory. "It's in the blood, I suppose. Skye, the home of the Mac-Leods. And the MacDonalds and the Mac-Kinnons."

"And the McCrimmons," ventured David.

"Oh, the McCrimmons too of course." The dimple was threatening an appearance.

"What are those islands between us and Skye?"

"The closest one is Muck. The big one on the left is Rum and the other, the one with the head-land, is Eigg."

"What odd names!"

"Odd? Oh, I suppose so. If you're accustomed to such sensible names as Medicine Hat or Moose Jaw."

David laughed. "*Touché,*" he said. "I see you know something about Canada even if you've never heard of Woodstock. Are those islands MacLeod country too?"

"No. Just MacDonalds there."

The sunlight was glowing on the crests of Sandy's hair as errant curls moved at the whim of the wind. Her cheeks and lips were weather flushed and more freckles seemed to have appeared at the touch of the sun. Beauty, beauty everywhere, thought David.

"Just MacDonalds," he echoed. "Seems to me I remember tales of battles and massacres."

"Battles and massacres? Yes, there were plenty of those. Though likely not as many as one might think. After all, that's all we hear about in history. We ignore the years in between. If there were any," she added, a little doubtfully. "Do you know what part of Skye your mother came from?"

"Not far from Dunvegan. The last address we had from her cousin was Portree. Where's your home, Sandy?"

She patted the rail affectionately. "This is my home. The *Bochan*. I was born on Skye, brought up on the mainland, lived in Edinburgh for a while. My parents were killed in an auto accident when I was ten and I came to live with Uncle Rory. We have a house in Calluig—that's our home port in Lewis where I lived when I was in school—but this is my real home." She turned and surveyed the little ship with the pride of ownership, then looked at David again. "We'll be going to Calluig after we deliver our cargo. Then you'll be going to see Ramshaw, will you?"

David nodded. "With you and Rory, I hope. I'm looking forward to my first castle. Ramshaw said something about it being the old home of the Morrisons."

"Aye. Morrison of Ramshaw used to be a powerful chieftain, but don't expect the Laird to tell you about it. He's not very interested in history. Of course if he was a Morrison himself it would likely be different. Speak to his man, Aulay MacLure, or go to his library. His father—Ramshaw's, I mean—had a wonderful collection of books about the Islands."

"He said that your uncle knows as much about the Islands as anyone."

"That's true. He could tell you all about the castle before we go."

"Good idea." David suddenly remembered the task Ramshaw had assigned him. This seemed like a good opportunity. "I suppose you've heard the rumours about strange submarines being sighted in this area?"

"Oh, we've heard them of course. At least about *one* strange submarine. It should be a great tourist attraction—like the Loch Ness Monster."

David laughed. "Have you ever seen it? What does your uncle think about it?"

"Ask him," she said.

But Rory's attention was directed elsewhere. He stood at the wheel, balancing effortlessly with the gentle roll of the ship, using only an occasional adjustment of the wheel to maintain course. He was holding binoculars to his eyes, looking southward. David and Sandy followed the direction of his gaze.

A trawler was approaching on a course that would eventually take her across their bow.

"What do you make of her, Uncle Rory?"

"She's flying a Swedish flag. I can't make out her name. Take the wheel for a minute, Sandy."

The trawler was steaming steadily, belching black smoke from her stack. White foam swirled at her bow and her wash spread out in streamers over the calm surface. She was perhaps a little smaller than the *Phantom,* David judged, turning his glasses on her, but she seemed to have plenty of power. Otherwise, as far as he could see she was like any other trawler.

"Is there anything unusual about her?" he asked.

"Her presence here is unusual." Rory moved

closer to his side at the rail. "The herring fleet left this area last week. They come over during the season, which is May and June. Yon trawler may have come with the Baltic fleet, but if so why didn't she leave with them?"

He paused and David focused his glasses again but still could not quite make out the name on the bow.

"We're naturally suspicious of trawlers here, David. The Minch, the body of water between the Inner and Outer Hebrides, is too shallow for trawling. These ships sweep the bottom and crush the young fish and break up the spawning grounds. But that doesn't worry some people. They come in under cover of darkness and make a quick haul, then run for it, not caring how much they spoil it for others."

"How should they go about it?"

"With fishing smacks and with trammel, drift or seine nets. Of course, trawlers are often used as cargo ships to take on the catch made by the wee boats. We have no quarrel with that. Your eyes are younger than mine, lad. Can you make out her name yet?"

"Almost. It's *Starvik,* I think. No, *Storvik.* That's it."

"*Storvik?*" Rory's forehead creased in thought, then cleared. "Oh, aye, I remember her now. She came over with the Baltic fleet all right." He lowered his glasses, reached for the whistle cord and blew two short blasts. "Swing her to port, Sandy."

As the *Bochan* heeled over the *Storvik* came on and passed close to starboard. A man leaned out of her wheelhouse and waved to them. Then she was past. The *Bochan* rocked gently in her wash.

Sandy readjusted their course and looked after the other ship. "Isn't she the one that ran aground on Scalpay, Uncle Rory?"

"Aye. She was caught in a gale and her skipper ran too close inshore. They were able to refloat themselves, but not before she suffered minor damage. Some of her crew were injured."

"Last I heard of her she was still in Tarbert."

"Aye. She was repaired there and some of her injured men recovered ashore, but it looks as if she's all set again. I wonder what she's doing down this way?"

"Taking a trial run in good weather, I expect," said Sandy. "You're too suspicious, Uncle."

Rory nodded, relieving Sandy at the wheel again. "Aye, I'm suspicious. Most of my friends are fishermen and I don't like to see trawlers spoiling their fishing grounds."

"Well, she wasn't trawling at that speed anyway." Sandy turned to rejoin David at the rail and remembered what they had been talking about before the *Storvik* had interrupted them. "Uncle Rory, David was wondering what you thought about those submarine rumours," she said.

"Well," answered Rory, considering, "I haven't seen any submarines myself, but I believe there's little doubt that there is one somewhere in the Hebrides that the Navy has claimed as its own. Or *was* anyway. I haven't heard of any recent sightings."

"Then it's just a Royal Navy submarine on manoeuvres?"

"So they would have us believe. But I've an idea they're just saying that to calm all us worriers."

"Why do you say that?"

Rory shrugged. "Just a feeling. First they denied it, then when rumours persisted they said it was a new K-class submarine on trials. But I've seen pictures of the K-class. Nothing new about this one from what I've heard."

"But I don't understand. What would a strange submarine be doing here?"

"Well, I'll tell you what I think, lad. I think it probably belongs to smugglers."

The idea of smugglers presented a very vivid picture in David's mind—a picture of briefly flashing signals on a moonless night, of muffled oars and blackened faces, of treasure chests and deep, dark caves. "They must be moving awfully valuable cargoes if they can afford their own sub," he said doubtfully.

"Aye. no doubt they are. But there's plenty of money in certain goods. Drugs, for instance. There are users and pushers all over the world and the person supplying them could afford anything."

"There are terrorists all over the world too," suggested Sandy. "Anyone smuggling arms could certainly afford a submarine."

David's romantic picture of old-time smugglers vanished abruptly. Drugs and arms. Ugly—and frightening. And John Edward Cairns had probably *not* died by accident... David shivered. Thank goodness his part in this mess was almost complete. There was just one more duty he had to perform for Ramshaw and this was his opening.

"Smugglers, eh? Well, if so, maybe that other rumour makes sense after all."

"What rumour would you be talking about?" asked Rory.

"The one about the base. Haven't you heard it? Apparently some people are saying there's not only a submarine but a base somewhere in the Hebrides too. But that's hardly possible, surely? I mean, there are lots of islands and I guess some of them are uninhabited, but there's also plenty of traffic. It would be pretty difficult to operate a base without someone knowing about it, wouldn't it?"

"Not at all," said Rory. "Especially with a submarine. It would be quite possible. I can think of several islands that would serve, with no one the wiser."

"All right," said Sandy, "where? If they hired you to suggest an island they could use as their base, which one would you pick?"

Thank you, Sandy, thought David. Just what I wanted to ask.

"That's quite a problem," said Rory. "There are actually hundreds of unoccupied islands." He waved his arm to encompass those in sight. "As David says, there is probably too much traffic here, even for a submarine. To be sure, such a base should be beyond the Outer Hebrides."

"St. Kilda?" suggested David. "Or the Flannans?"

"Aye, those are possibilities. However, you wouldn't have to go that far out if you didn't want to. Just a minute while I fetch a map."

He was back quickly with a map which they held open together. "There are many places that could be used for such a purpose without too much fixing up. But there's one place that would require very little fixing, if any. It has a natural harbour with an entrance that's almost invisible. Only when sailing close in to the cliffs can you see the opening and there's seldom any reason to do that. That's it there."

David's heart skipped a beat. Rory was pointing to Sgeir Dubh, Black Rock Island. What would Ramshaw think of that?

Rory continued. "As you can see, it's remote, away from the mainland and from inhabited islands and shipping lanes. And yet it's only a short run from Uist. There's a natural cave in the hillside that could be easily enlarged if necessary and a wee lochan to provide sheltered anchorage."

"Sgeir Dubh," said Sandy. "I knew you'd pick that."

"Aye. Sandy and I are two of the very few people who know anything about the place. Others know it's there, of course. You can't miss its rocky cliffs. But I can count on my fingers the number of people who know there's a passage into a lochan there."

"Why is that?"

Rory shrugged. "There's no cause for anyone

to go there except maybe the odd bird watcher now and then. There's nothing to suggest that it is anything more than a black sea rock as the name implies. However, there is an old book that tells the story of the island. I've seen a copy and because of it Sandy and I went in close to the cliffs and in through the entrance. Would you like to hear the story?"

"Very much."

"It goes back to the year 1746, after the battle of Culloden. As you no doubt know, Bonnie Prince Charlie was in flight from Bloody Cumberland, with a price on his head. Many Highlanders sheltered him in those times, lad. Three of them were the Conuil brothers. They hid him for a time, then passed him on to friends when the search became too hot. The Conuils themselves were taken prisoner and marched off to Fort William. Somehow along the way the three brothers escaped and fled to the Isles with Cumberland's men on their heels. Some points in the story are not very clear, but in one way or another the three men reached Sgeir Dubh. Whether they knew of it beforehand or landed there by chance, I don't know. However, the redcoats followed them, found the opening to the lochan and searched the island from keel to crow's-nest, but found no trace of the Conuils. And yet, as they were sailing away there were the three men standing on the cliff top, waving to them, laughing at them. The soldiers returned but the same thing happened again. The Highlanders disappeared as before."

"Is this a true story or just a legend?"

"Legend can be founded on fact. The man who wrote the book believed it to be true but had no explanation. Some say the fairies took pity on the brothers and hid them away in their underground homes when the soldiers came. But I'm sure you won't be putting much faith in Highland superstition. General opinion was that there was a cave somewhere and they hid in it. Conuil's Cave it has been called, though no one knows where it is."

"Including us," said Sandy. "We looked for it when we went there. We found a cave in the hillside above the lochan, but that wouldn't be it. The soldiers could hardly have missed it. I expect we're the only ones who've been ashore there in years. The story seems to be pretty well forgotten."

"Perhaps David will bring us luck. Would you like to go to Sgeir Dubh with us sometime soon and have another look for Conuil's Cave?"

"Sure would," said David. Everything was working out better than he could have hoped. He had a report for Ramshaw; his part in the affair was over. Now he could sit back and enjoy the fruits of his effort: the *Island Phantom,* Ramshaw Castle, Black Rock Island.

If only he could forget John Edward Cairns.

5

Ramshaw Castle was a gloomy stone-and-lime stronghold. It stood at the top of a long rise, with a headland looming behind it and moorland rolling away on three sides. The Laird's car crossed a tumbling stream and moved up the hedge-lined driveway.

"Here we are." Ramshaw slipped out from behind the wheel and hurried around to open the door for the others. "I'll show you to your rooms and you can change if you like. I'm only sorry that Rory couldn't come as well, but I understand. Sandy, you're the first lady to dine in Ramshaw since my mother was here. MacLure is the happiest man in Scotland tonight."

The Laird turned to David. "Aulay MacLure and his wife look after the house for me. Aulay is my butler, footman and goodness knows what all, as well as being my official piper." He grinned. "As Laird of Ramshaw I'm expected to have an official piper. At least Aulay expects it. I think he still regards us Fletchers as interlopers—even wears the Morrison tartan instead of ours. His ambition for years has been to arrange another dinner in the great hall, so that's where we'll dine tonight." He opened a door leading into the newer part of the house and ushered his guests into a long hallway.

Sandy looked around at the wide, sweeping stairway and the doors leading off the hallway. "What do you do with a house this size?" she asked. "You must feel like the last herring in the net."

Ramshaw laughed. "I don't notice the size, lass. I have a room upstairs and a bunk in my den as well, and that's often as far as I go. I rarely even have the inclination to unpack when I come here. Look." He indicated a cupboard at the foot of the staircase in which stood five blue suitcases. "Still packed since I left London last month. I'll soon be taking them back again, probably unopened. I hate fuss and bother."

He led the way upstairs and stopped before the first door on the right. "MacLure wanted to meet you but I told him to stay with the dinner. This will be your room, David. Dinner will be served in about half an hour—you'll hear MacLure playing the pipes. Follow the sound and you'll find your way to the dining room. Sandy, you room is farther along."

Half an hour later the wail of the pipes led David to the great hall. He paused in the stone-arched doorway.

A hundred candles and a leaping fire lit the room, touching the cold grey stones of floor and walls with a warm glow. Shadows lurked in the far corners and among the rafters overhead. Over the fireplace a pair of ancient claymores winked back the candlelight, and on the opposite wall the glassy eyes of a stag's head burned red.

A massive table ran the length of the room. Most of it was bare except for the glittering candlesticks that stood at intervals along it. At the far end, close to the fireplace, were settings for three.

An old man with white hair and a sprightly step was marching around the table. The light sparkled on the jewelled clasp at his shoulder and the polished ornaments on his sporran. The buckles of his shoes winked as he trod the worn flagstones. The cry of his pipes echoed through the vaulted room.

"It's like stepping into the past."

David felt a hand on his arm and turned. Sandy stood there wearing a rust-coloured dress of French silk, radiant in the firelight that touched her hair and shone in the depths of her eyes.

"That's MacLure playing the pipes," she said. "For goodness sakes, will you look at this place!"

David looked at her instead. "It's hard to believe you're a deck hand on a trawler," he said.

She laughed and hugged his arm. "Tonight I'm a lady. Tonight I'm 'The MacLeod,' chief of the clan, and yonder is my piper. He's playing 'Miss MacLeod's Reel.'" Her foot was tapping. "Could you dance to that, Davie?"

"If you were my teacher, I could. Here's Ramshaw coming."

The Laird entered at another door. He should have been wearing a kilt, thought David, and tartan hose and buckled shoes. Instead he wore a rough tweed jacket and trousers. But the atmosphere had touched him nonetheless. He paused before them and bowed, then offered his arm to Sandy.

"This is a great day for Ramshaw Castle, Miss MacLeod. We haven't seen such a beautiful lady at our table since my mother was here. What do you say, McCrimmon?"

"I'm sure of it," David replied, aware of his inadequacy.

"Thank you, kind sirs," said Sandy with a curtsy. "You are both very gallant—and very much full of the blarney."

"Not at all," protested the Laird. "It's true, every word of it. I don't know how the old house will behave, it's been so long since there was a lady present. But MacLure hasn't forgotten how things should be done, at any rate. He'll go on blowing those things all night if we don't sit down, so come along."

MacLure came to a halt behind the Laird's chair and completed the tune he was playing. "It was good to hear the pipes at dinnertime again, MacLure." The Laird turned to the old man. "I didn't recognize the tunes, though."

"They were in honour of our guests, sir. 'Miss MacLeod's Reel' and 'McCrimmon's Lament.'"

Ramshaw smiled. "Very appropriate, though I hope we don't give McCrimmon any cause to lament. You have met Sandy—pardon me, Miss MacLeod—I believe?"

"Aye. It is a pleasure to serve a beautiful lady, Miss MacLeod."

"And this is McCrimmon—David McCrimmon from Canada."

David stood and extended his hand to the old man. The hand that clasped his was firm and strong. "Welcome to the Isles, sir, and to Ramshaw. It is an honour to play for a McCrimmon. Some of the greatest pipers in the history of Scotland were McCrimmons, you know."

"Thank you. I've been overwhelmed by my welcome. I enjoyed your playing, Mr. MacLure."

It was a delightful interlude that followed. As the fire died down the shadows thickened and the brooding grey walls drew in. The eyes of the stag's head burned bright as coals in the gloom. MacLure hovered in the background, now and then moving about soundlessly. The magic of the moorland was in the air and on the table. There was salmon from the burn, roast fowl and venison from the heathered slopes, vegetables from the fields behind the house.

But David soon lost track of the food, there was such variety. He was more conscious of the great hall, of the sense of endless time that seemed to reach down out of eternity and touch them. And of Sandy. The glow of the candlelight was warm on her cheeks and on the fire in her hair. Her long lashes shadowed her eyes except when she looked across at him, and then the light was in them too, warm and sparkling. He was disappointed when the Laird pushed back his chair, indicating that the meal was over.

"Now, if you're sure you've had enough to eat, Miss MacLeod," he said, "David and I are going to leave you for a few minutes. We're reliving tradition tonight and it's tradition for the gentlemen to retire for drinks after a meal and leave the ladies to their own devices. I'm sorry."

"Oh no, you go right ahead. I don't want to spoil anything. But perhaps you would show me where the library is."

"Certainly. MacLure will take you there and we'll join you in about half an hour. Now, David, will you come this way?"

A few minutes later David found himself in Ramshaw's den in the old tower. It was a complete contrast to the great hall where they had eaten. The grey stone walls were like those in the hall, but here they were lighted by electricity. A radio transmitter stood opposite the door. On one wall hung a huge map of Scotland and the surrounding islands. Below it were two telephones and a man seated in a deep chair. He wore the uniform of a Naval Commander.

"Ah, Greg, I'm glad you made it. This is David McCrimmon, the lad I told you about. David, Commander Stanley."

"I've heard all about your experience." The Commander stood up and shook David's hand. He was short and slim and gave the impression of competence. "We're grateful to you."

David nodded, his attention drawn to the two telephones. "A hot line?" he asked, grinning.

"Not far off the mark," Ramshaw replied. "The one on the right is a regular telephone on the Stornoway exchange; the other is a direct connection with dockside in Stornoway. With Commander Stanley, or his aides if he's not there."

He motioned David to a chair, jabbed a switch that rang a distant bell and sat down behind a big desk. "There's a destroyer in Stornoway, *HMS Audax*. The Navy has put her at our disposal until we've cleared this matter up—which gives you an idea of the seriousness with which the authorities regard it. Commander Stanley is our liaison with *Audax*. Greg and the skipper of the destroyer are the only ones who know why she's here."

Now Commander Stanley turned to David. "You were going to sound out Rory MacLeod on the submarine rumours."

"Yes, sir. He's heard them, of course, and believes there's at least some truth in them. Doesn't seem to worry him though."

"I see. Has he any theories on the subject?"

"His guess is that the submarine is being used by smugglers. Possibly drugs or arms."

Ramshaw and the Commander exchanged significant glances but neither commented.

"And were you able to bring up—Just a minute." Ramshaw held up his hand for silence as a discreet rap on the door preceded the entrance of MacLure bearing a tray of drinks.

"Thanks, MacLure. Just leave the tray here. Are you looking after Miss MacLeod?"

"Aye, sir, she's in the library reading."

"Fine. I won't be needing you anymore tonight. Just look after the young lady. Goodnight, MacLure."

"Yes, sir. Goodnight." MacLure nodded to each of the three and withdrew.

"Now," said Ramshaw, "where were we? Oh,

yes. Were you able to broach the subject of a base to Rory, David?"

"Yes. That was no problem. He said there's one island that would be ideal. Away from major shipping lanes yet reasonably close to the other islands, with an almost invisible entrance to a small loch and even a ready-made cave in the hillside."

"Sounds as if it's made to order," said the Commander. "Where is it? Has it a name?"

"Yes. I don't know how you'll like this," he said to Ramshaw, "but it's the same one your agent, John Cairns, drew on his map. Sgeir Dubh."

"It is, eh?" Ramshaw drummed his fingers on the desk, then turned to the Commander. "Are you familiar with it?"

"I'm not familiar with it, no. I know where it is and what it looks like but I've never had cause to go ashore, or even to go nearby."

The Commander stepped over to the map on the wall; the other two joined him. He located Sgeir Dubh and stood there, his fingertip marking it while he surveyed the rest of the map. "If Rory MacLeod says this would be the most appropriate island for a clandestine submarine base, then I take it we have our answer?"

"Well," said Ramshaw slowly, "that could be one argument against its use. If you want a secret base you don't pick the obvious."

"But I gather it's only obvious to those who are familiar with it. And how many might that be?"

"Very few, I think," ventured David. "Rory says it's almost unknown."

"In which case," said Ramshaw, "how would the smugglers—if that's what they are—know about it?"

"No doubt they have their ways. If they can operate a submarine we can't underestimate their abilities in other directions. The question is, is Sulsted familiar with Sgeir Dubh?"

"Sulsted?" David looked perplexed. "You mean the bird man?"

Ramshaw hesitated, then shrugged. "Since it's out, yes, you might as well know. We're sure Professor Sulsted is the brains behind this whole matter."

"Sulsted! For heaven's sake!" David remembered the little man with the crossed eyes rebuking him in Tobermory for his lack of knowledge about gulls. Surely if there was ever a harmless little man . . .

"Did you suspect him when we met him in Tobermory?"

"I have suspected him myself for a long time, and Cairns' note to me on the map confirmed my suspicions. Remember it said 'We are right about X'? Well, Sulsted is X. Apparently Cairns came across evidence to support my theory. Since I learned that, I've let Greg and the rest of MI5 know about my suspicions. I've had Sulsted under close surveillance since Tobermory, but we haven't arrested him yet. We're hoping he'll lead us to the answer to this whole riddle if we give him enough rope. This," he said to David gravely, "is strictly confidential. Actually I shouldn't be telling you all this, but after what you've done to help us I feel we owe you something."

"I won't breathe a word, of course."

"Good. Now as Greg says, could Sulsted possibly know the secret of Sgeir Dubh? As a bird fancier it's just the type of island you might expect him to explore but what's strange is that apparently he has never done so. Since we began to suspect him I've had him followed everywhere and we've traced many of his previous moves. He has been to a number of islands, ostensibly as a bird watcher, but he has never been to Sgeir Dubh. There is no doubt on that score whatever. So how could he know about it?"

"Doesn't seem likely," admitted the Commander.

"No, it doesn't. And we have reason to believe that the submarine base is in another area entirely. Probably in the Orkneys—where, incidentally, Sulsted *has* been seen more than once."

"The Orkneys?" David found the group of islands on the map. "Away up there?"

"I've never heard of any sightings up there," commented the Commander.

"Exactly," agreed Ramshaw. "My hunch is that the known sightings have been intentional. I think the smugglers have purposely permitted us to catch a glimpse of the submarine down this way so we won't be nosing around the northern area."

"A good theory, Ramshaw. So you suggest we ignore MacLeod's choice of Sgeir Dubh?"

Ramshaw hesitated. "We don't *ignore* it," he

said. "We don't ignore anything Rory says about the Hebrides. Many times I've seriously considered taking him into our confidence and making use of his knowledge. In fact, if we had evidence that Sulsted was familiar with that island, or that he was even aware of its suitability, I'd send the *Audax* down there first thing in the morning. As it is"—he shrugged—"I think we look elsewhere."

"Well, that's up to you," said Commander Stanley. "The *Audax* is ready to go at a moment's notice whether it's to Sgeir Dubh, the Orkneys or the South Pole."

"Yes, I know. But the treasury takes a dim view of it if I send her anywhere without good solid reasons for doing so." Ramshaw puffed on his pipe in silence for a moment, contemplating the map hanging before him. Then he turned his back on it.

"Well, David, I told you there was only one more thing I wanted you to do after you got yourself mixed up in this affair. You've done it admirably. Now you must no longer concern yourself. It's up to Commander Stanley and myself and a few other professionals. At the appropriate time I intend to tell the authorities what you've done and I have no doubt you'll be hearing from them. I assure you they will be grateful. But for now you're out of it."

"That's a relief."

"I told Sandy I'd see her in half an hour," continued the Laird, "but I'm afraid I won't. Greg and I have some important business to discuss. So if you don't mind I'm going to leave you to entertain her. Ask MacLure for anything you want. You'll find her in the library at the far end of the hall."

Sandy was stretched out on a chesterfield, a book propped in front of her. "Hi," she said as he came in. "Where's the Laird?"

David didn't answer her question. "Good heavens!" he said. "Look at all the books!" He was surrounded by them. They reached from floor to ceiling on all sides except where the door, window and fireplace were. "How did you ever pick out *one* book to read from all of these?"

"Oh, that was easy." She sat up, tucking her feet under her skirt to make room for him. "I asked MacLure to show me where the books about the Hebrides were. There are four solid rows of them, some quite old and rare. I picked out two, one for each of us. Is Ramshaw coming?"

"No. He sends his apologies but he has a visitor and they have some business to discuss. He thought maybe you and I could entertain each other."

"Good. I may sound ungrateful but I'm glad he's not coming. He isn't interested in the old books at all—or even in the story of his own castle."

"How come there are so many here if Ramshaw isn't interested in them?"

"I think they came with the castle when his father bought it. *He* was interested but the present Laird isn't. Mind you, he would be if he realized how valuable some of them are. I've heard he's a real connoisseur of valuable pieces of art, like those candlesticks on the table at dinner and some of the pictures in the hall. But not books." She sighed. "I just wish he'd get rid of them and give them to me."

"You'd have to build an extra deck on the *Bochan* if he did that."

"That's true. Well, I'd be happy if he just gave me my choice of a dozen. These are two I would choose." She indicated the one she was reading and the other that she had selected for him. "This is yours. *History and Legend in the Hebrides.* It tells about Sgeir Dubh and Conuil's Cave. Uncle Rory first read about it in another copy of this same book. It's the only one that seems to tell the whole story."

"It must be just legend then, don't you think? Still, it will be interesting reading. What's your book?"

"*The Morrisons of Ramshaw.*" She showed him the book. "I'm interested even if Ramshaw isn't. It's mostly about the Morrisons—just mentions briefly that the present Laird's father finally bought the land."

But David wasn't really listening to her. Instead, he watched the leaping flames in the fireplace, felt the warmth on his face, followed the flickering of the shadows across the ceiling. And mostly he was aware of the shades and highlights on Sandy's face and in her hair, of her long lashes and the soft curve of her lips. She was just as comfortable here, he thought, as barefoot on the deck of a trawler, as much at home in a castle, among tiers of books, as on the bridge of the *Bochan* in a rising gale.

Sandy turned back to her book and David picked up *History and Legend in the Hebrides*. As he did so it fell open and a torn piece of newspaper dropped out. The heading on the page caught his eye: *Conuil's Cave.*

"Thanks for marking the place for me."

"Pardon?" Sandy looked up, curious. "But I didn't mark it. I didn't open the book at all."

"Oh? Must be a coincidence then. There's a marker in the book right at the chapter on Conuil's Cave." He looked at it more carefully. It had been torn carelessly from a newspaper, fairly recently by the look of it. On one side was an advertisement for tires; on the other was an account of the funeral of a Doctor Gordon of Stornoway. The dateline was missing.

He showed it to Sandy. "Any idea how long ago that was?"

"That must be from the *Post,*" she said. "Doctor Gordon died about four weeks ago. Maybe five." She looked at David questioningly.

"Just wondering," he said casually. "You say the Laird doesn't read these books much but apparently someone has been reading this particular one since Doctor Gordon's funeral."

"That's right. I expect it must have been MacLure," she continued slowly. "If he was reading about Sgeir Dubh he might be interested to know that we're planning to go there to search for the cave. We'll ask him when he comes—he's going to bring us some tea later."

David would have liked to talk to MacLure right away but suppressed his impatience and turned to his book.

A half hour later Sandy finally sat up and reached for the bell switch. "I don't know about you," she said, "but I can't wait any longer for my tea. Will it be all right if I summon MacLure now?" She grinned. "Summon. Doesn't that sound grand?"

David was relieved. "Sure, go ahead. Summon away."

MacLure himself gave David the opening he was hoping for as he wheeled a tea table before them and removed the cloth to reveal a teapot in a cosy and a plate of cookies. "It's good to see someone reading those old books again. I hope you're enjoying them."

"Very much. I suppose you read them a great deal yourself?"

MacLure smiled. "Not those particular ones, Mr. McCrimmon. I am well acquainted with the Islands and the information in those books. I don't believe I've opened them in years but I like to come in here now and then just to sit. It's like being among old friends."

David glanced at Sandy. She raised her eyebrows, slightly puzzled. He picked up the scrap of paper and held it out. "I gathered that the old books aren't read very often, but I found this in one of them—looks as if someone used it for a marker."

MacLure fumbled for a pair of glasses and adjusted them on his nose. His eyebrows rose in surprise. "Doctor Gordon. A month ago or a little more. I didn't think anyone had been reading in here since then."

"The Laird, perhaps," suggested David.

MacLure shook his head. "The old Laird loved them. The first of the Fletchers, I mean. But the present Laird has no interest in them—he was aye his mother's bairn." He sighed. "She was not a Scot. The old Laird brought her here from one of those foreign lands but she hated it, especially when she found out he hadn't as much money as she'd expected." The old man suddenly looked shocked and glanced anxiously at David. "I'm— I'm sorry. You'll pay no attention to the ramblings of an old man." He removed his glasses and put them back in his pocket with trembling fingers.

David sat in embarrassed silence while tea was poured. Then he resolutely took up the subject again. "I wonder who could have been reading the book."

Sandy looked at him in surprise, but the question had a steadying effect on MacLure. "I wonder. It wouldn't be the Laird and there has been no one—" He hesitated. David glanced at him hopefully. "There *was* someone who spent an hour or two in here and it would be just about the time of the doctor's death. But I don't think—"

"Who was it, Mr. MacLure?"

"I don't remember his name. He came to see the Laird but he was out and I wasn't expecting him for some time. The man asked if he could wait and I put him in here. Aye, and I gave him the newspaper to read while he was waiting too."

"Did he see the Laird?" David didn't dare look at Sandy, who was obviously puzzled by his insistence.

"No, sir. When I came back later to tell him the Laird was on his way he had already gone. I don't believe he ever came back either. Of course he may have met the Laird at another time."

"What did he look like?"

"He was a wee man. There was something very odd about his eyes."

David sat up abruptly.

Sandy spoke first. "That sounds like Professor Sulsted. You wouldn't know him, David."

But David knew him all right. Sulsted. The man behind the smuggling ring and the submarine. X. And the little professor had been reading about Sgeir Dubh.

"Aye," MacLure was saying, "I believe that was the name. Sulsted. He was saying something about birds."

David drummed his fingers on the arm of the chesterfield. What was it Ramshaw had said? That if he knew Sulsted was familiar with Black Rock Island he would probably send *HMS Audax* down there first thing in the morning. And evidently Sulsted *was* familiar with it. The story in the book told of the concealed loch, of the cave in the hillside . . .

He stood up. "If you'll excuse me, I'll be back in a minute."

He went out quickly, down the long hallway to where the iron-bound door led to Ramshaw's den. But there he paused.

Perhaps there was no real urgency. The Laird was busy with the Commander and might not welcome an interruption. David had been dismissed after all—taken off the case, so to speak.

Nothing much could be done tonight anyway. He would report what he had learned first thing in the morning and Ramshaw could make of it what he pleased. In the meantime he was supposed to entertain Sandy. Morning would be time enough.

6

David awoke to be informed that Ramshaw had been called away sometime during the night. MacLure was able to tell him only that the Laird was apologetic and trusted that his guests would entertain themselves until his return at noon.

Under more relaxed circumstances David would have enjoyed the wait. Sandy was taking an interest in everything about the old castle, exploring and engaging MacLure in reminiscences. David joined in, but only half-heartedly. He wished he had gone ahead the night before and reported what he had discovered. He remembered the telephone in the Laird's den, the one connected directly with Commander Stanley's office in Stornoway, but discreet checking disclosed that it was inaccessible behind a locked door. He could only wait and hope.

And then new word came from Ramshaw. Profuse apologies, but he had been called to London and would not be able to return until the next day at the earliest. He would make it up to his guests at a later date. At David's insistence

MacLure tried to contact Ramshaw at his London office but was unable to reach him.

Unseeing, David stared out the window of his room, his packed knapsack beside him. He had blundered. It was all very well to say that his part in the affair was over and done with. But it wasn't. Not while he had information that might affect Ramshaw's plans a great deal.

He sat on the edge of the bed and tried to recall all that had been said in the tower room the previous night. Ramshaw had definitely stated that if he had reason to believe Sulsted was familiar with the advantages of Black Rock Island as a submarine base the *Audax* would be sent there immediately to investigate.

David tried to convince himself that withholding his discovery until Ramshaw's return would probably make little difference, but the rationalizing didn't work. He had the uneasy feeling that it might very well mean the difference between the success or failure of the campaign against the smugglers.

Well, it was too late now to stew about his inaction last night, he decided. There was only one thing to do: leave a message for Ramshaw and hope the delay wouldn't make a crucial difference.

He wrote the message, sealed it and gave it to MacLure with a request to pass it on to Ramshaw as soon as the Laird returned. His note of thanks, he explained, for Ramshaw's hospitality.

* * *

David and Sandy sat in the *Island Phantom's*

wardroom having lunch with Rory. David had had a brief chance to thank Adam again for arranging his trip on the *Phantom* and to learn that an inquest seemed unlikely. After Adam returned to the engine room Sandy told her uncle all about the castle. She mentioned that Ramshaw had a copy of the book relating the story of Sgeir Dubh and Conuil's Cave.

"Well now, I was just thinking," said Rory, "that this would be as good a time as any to pay our visit to that island."

David looked up sharply. Not now! Not until the *Audax* had a chance to get there first. Suppose the smugglers *were* there and the *Phantom* stumbled onto their secret. People who dealt illegally in drugs or arms weren't to be taken lightly. And even if we don't find the smugglers, he reasoned, we might accidentally tip them off and make them leave before the crew of the *Audax* could nab them.

"Now?" He tried to sound casual. "You mean today?"

"Aye. We'll be sailing in half an hour. We'll be there before nightfall and we could stay over and explore the island tomorrow. Actually we're on our way to Barra, but when we get there is no one's business but our own. Why, lad? Was there something else you were wanting to do today?"

"No." David was aware that they were both looking at him with curious expressions. How was he going to prevent this trip? What could he say to at least delay it until Ramshaw had received his message?

Suddenly he remembered something else Ramshaw had said the night before in the tower room: that many times he had been tempted to take Rory into his confidence in order to make use of his intimate knowledge of the Hebrides. There was no other way. Ramshaw would forgive him.

David drew in a deep breath. "I guess I'll have to tell you the whole story."

"The whole story?" They were both puzzled. "What story?"

As he told them they listened intently, Rory with his dead pipe clenched between his teeth, Sandy with comprehension dawning in her eyes.

"I thought you were acting strangely." She was the first to speak. "You were so determined to know who had been reading that book and this morning you were so insistent that MacLure try to contact Ramshaw. But Sulsted? Are you sure Sulsted is the man?"

"Aye," added Rory, "that's hard to believe. I like the wee man." He lit his pipe with slow deliberation.

"Well now," he said at last between puffs, "let me see if we have understood you. Military Intelligence is after this submarine. They have proof that Sulsted is the brains behind the operation, whatever it is—and I don't know what it could be other than smuggling—but they aren't sure where the base is."

"Right," replied David.

"Why don't they just arrest Sulsted and get the information from him?" asked Sandy.

"Aye, that would seem the quickest way of doing it," nodded Rory. "But no doubt they've thought of that so there must be good reasons why they don't do it. Perhaps they can't take Sulsted without the rest of his crowd being aware of it and having time to escape. What Ramshaw wants to know, as I see it, is whether or not Sgeir Dubh is being used as the base, so they can close in on the whole operation when they take Sulsted. Now there," he said, "we can help."

"But I don't think Ramshaw would want you to," said David quickly. "The reason I told you all this after I promised not to tell anyone was to prevent you from going down there. I mean, he wouldn't want you risking yourselves or the *Phantom* doing something the *Audax* is supposed to do."

Rory waved that aside. "If it meant going into danger, lad, I wouldn't do it. At least not without explaining the situation to the crew and getting their consent. But I don't think there's any danger. All you really know right now is that Sulsted is aware of the possibilities of Sgeir Dubh as a submarine base. But if you can report to Ramshaw or Commander Stanley tomorrow that someone *is* there, using the island for whatever purpose, wouldn't that be more helpful to them?"

"Oh, I'm sure it would. But how can we know that without actually going ashore and tipping off the smugglers?"

Rory grinned. "The birds, lad—Sulsted's birds —they'll tell us. The birds nesting in those cliffs probably haven't been disturbed in years. If there has been a submarine coming and going and men walking about the island the birds will tell us by their actions. We'll simply sail by, not too closely, and we'll be able to see whether or not anyone has been ashore in the last little while."

David laughed, pleased. "As simple as that. Wouldn't it be ironic if Sulsted's gulls gave him away?"

"Well," said Sandy, heading for the door, "if we're sailing in half an hour there are things to be done. This is going to be exciting. Imagine being mixed up in this kind of—" As she opened the door Adam Brieve stumbled into the room. "Adam! You startled me!"

"Sorry." Adam recovered himself quickly. "I just came to report that the engines are warmed up and we can sail at any time."

"Right. Thank you, Adam," said Rory. "Twenty minutes then. We're heading south for Barra but we'll sail a wee bit to the west to show David the Monach Islands."

"Aye, aye, sir." Adam touched his cap and disappeared.

Sandy looked after his retreating figure with a frown. "Uncle Rory," she said gravely, "he was listening at the door. I'm sure of it."

"Nonsense. Why would he do that? Away with you, lass, and no more of your havering. Just because we're heading out for a little amateur spying is no reason to suspect people of eavesdropping. Only twenty minutes before we sail."

*   *   *

The *Island Phantom* was doing her best to make good use of the last hours of daylight. She bit into the long swell, tossing a white mane back across the forecastle and bridge. The sky was overcast. North Uist was just visible as a cloud bank on the port quarter, merging seas with sky. Ahead were the Monach Islands and somewhere beyond them, Sgeir Dubh—Black Rock Island.

Rory was below for a belated supper so Sandy was at the wheel. David stood at the windscreen, peering through binoculars at the grey Atlantic ahead. It was so simple, he was telling himself. All they had to do was pass close enough to the cliffs to see if the birds had been disturbed. Nothing to it. Nothing that would arouse suspicion in anyone who might be up on the cliffs watching them.

He shivered in the freshening wind, but instead of going below for an extra sweater he put on one of the life jackets kept handy on the bridge. He drew the belt tighter as another surge of spray hit the wheelhouse. It was so simple, he repeated to himself. And yet, for some reason he felt uneasy. I guess I'm just scared, he thought.

"David, is there another life jacket over there?" Sandy broke into his reverie. "It's colder than I thought."

David handed one to her.

"Take the wheel for a minute while I put it on," she said. "No better time to learn to steer a ship."

David held the wheel and immediately felt the power of the sea as the swell hit them on the starboard bow, lifting the little ship, thrusting against the rudder.

"Keep your eyes on the compass," Sandy said. "That line represents the ship's head. See how you've gone off course? Swing the wheel back. No, no; not so fast. There, see, the ship's swinging. You have to come back to meet her. Oh, well. After all, it is your first time."

The next few minutes were some of the best David could remember. He felt exhilaration as the ship responded to his turns on the wheel, and gradually he overcame the wide variations that the ship's head showed at first on the gyrocompass. Looking back over his shoulder he could see the broad wake that traced their course over the restless water—it was definitely improving. And Sandy was a good teacher, resisting the impulse to take the wheel from him when at first he had trouble getting the hang of it.

"For an inlander you're not all that bad, Davie," she conceded. "We'll make a helmsman of you yet. It must be the Hebridean blood in your veins."

David grinned, accepting her comment as high praise. "Thank you," he said. "It's just as well Rory's been below though."

"But I haven't," said Rory, coming up the ladder. "I've been at the stern watching the wake. I knew fine it wasn't Sandy at the wheel. But you're coming along, lad."

He walked to the windscreen, adjusting his binoculars. "If it was a clear day we could see Sgeir Dubh by now. As it is we'll not be close enough for another ten, fifteen minutes. Visibility is closing in."

He came over to the wheel. "Thanks, lad. I'll take over now. If you would like a cup of tea, the men have the kettle on the boil down in the galley."

David left the bridge and started aft. As he passed the engine room hatch he thought about Adam Brieve—Adam, who may have been listening at the door when he was telling Rory all about the submarine affair.

Had he been listening? And if so, what did it mean? David remembered the man coming out of the mists at the foot of the cliff where John Edward Cairns lay dead. Running, as if he expected to find something—or someone. He couldn't have heard the cry that attracted me, David recalled. Was it just coincidence that he came along at that particular time? Or was he, just possibly, expecting to find a dead man there, expecting to search the body for who knows what?

Could Adam know that Cairns said something before he died, made me promise to deliver the map? David wondered. He remembered how closely he had been watched during the interview at the police station, particularly when the cut boot lace had been mentioned. And later, at the hotel, Adam had come in briefly and then abruptly gone out again. David remembered it very clearly. Adam had paused right by the coat rack, and somehow the map had changed pockets. Had Adam taken it out with him, then returned it to the wrong pocket?

Suddenly David felt a shiver run down his back. If his assumptions were correct, Adam must have watched him on board the *Skerryvore* to see who recognized the gull's feather and made contact with him. Ramshaw. Would that have been a surprise to him? What good would it do him to know? Would he warn Sulsted? For surely, if there were any truth in David's suspicions, it meant that Adam was one of the smugglers. Did he suggest I sail on the *Phantom* just so he could keep an eye on me? David mused. In case, just in case, John Edward Cairns *did* tell me something?

Adam. He probably knew right now that they were sailing close to Sgeir Dubh to ascertain whether or not someone was using the island as a base. If not, then no harm done. But if someone was there?

Quickly David turned and climbed back up to the bridge. But before he spoke Rory said, pointing, "There she is, lad, Sgeir Dubh."

Black Rock Island rose off the port bow, looming larger and larger, its sheer rocky cliffs sweeping abruptly out of the sea. David joined the others beside the wheel and turned his glasses on the island. It stood like some mediaeval castle, the waves beating ceaselessly at its cold ramparts.

And the sea birds wheeled and soared about the lofty turrets.

"Well," said Rory significantly, lowering his glasses, "there's your answer, David. They should be on their nests at this time of day. Something has disturbed them."

David nodded. He felt a surge of triumph. But his mouth was suddenly dry.

"It couldn't be anything else?" he asked.

"Oh, it *could* be," conceded Rory, "but the likelihood is very remote. That someone else should visit this island now, after all these years, would be just too much of a coincidence. But that's not our worry, lad. You left your message for Ramshaw. As soon as we reach Barra you can telephone him, and if he hasn't already sent the *Audax* to investigate, he will now."

David was studying the island through his glasses. "There's probably someone up there looking at us right now," he said.

"Very likely," nodded Rory. "So we'll not give them any cause to get suspicious. We'll change course away from the island and sail west. Since the channel to the lochan is on the east side that should reassure them."

David nodded. But he wasn't happy. If Adam had indeed been listening at the door . . .

"Rory," he said, "what do you know about Adam Brieve? I mean, have you known him for very long?"

"Adam?" Rory was surprised. "You haven't been letting Sandy's claim that he was eavesdropping give you any strange ideas about him, have you?"

"Maybe," admitted David. "But it's not just that. There are so many other things, little things. I'm beginning to wonder if he might be one of the smugglers."

"You're serious?" Rory looked at David closely. "What 'little things'?"

David told Rory what he'd been thinking just moments earlier. Before Rory could respond, Sandy spoke. "You must admit, Uncle, it was quite a coincidence that Adam was right there just when we needed a new engineer."

Rory nodded slowly, doubtfully. "Our former

engineer was hurt in a hit-and-run car accident, lad," he explained. "The driver has never been caught. That would be about five weeks ago. We had to have an engineer right away since we had a contract to carry goods between Mallaig and Uist. Adam turned up at just the right time. But we can't condemn a man for that. He's a good engineer with good references and that was our only worry at the time. I don't really think—" He stopped suddenly. He stiffened and frowned. "Now what?"

It was a moment before David realized what had happened. The deck was suddenly dead beneath their feet. The vibration had stopped.

There was an abrupt silence, then Rory barked into the engine-room voice pipe. "Adam! What's the matter?"

No reply. Suddenly the deck was alive again. The ship shuddered and the wake seethed. The engines had been thrown into reverse.

"Adam! *Mac an diabhol.* What's going on?"

"Uncle Rory!" It was Sandy, her voice high with excitement. "Look there."

David and Rory followed the direction of her pointing finger.

"Good Lord!" whispered Rory.

A submarine was emerging from the sea, her conning tower just breaking the surface. They watched, fascinated, dumbfounded, as she settled on an even keel, water cascading off her rounded hull. No markings showed on her black flanks. Immediately men appeared on her bridge.

Rory turned to the voice pipe again, his eyes

never leaving the submarine. "Adam!" he snapped. "Engine room! Answer me!"

No reply.

"Sandy," he said tensely, "see who you can raise on the wireless. David, go down there and tell Adam I want him. Now."

The two ran. David shot down the ladder from the bridge; his hands burned on the rails, his feet never touched the steps. As he reached the deck he heard a voice coming through a loudspeaker. For a moment he was stunned, then he realized— it had to be from the submarine.

"Ahoy, *Island Phantom*. Ahoy, Rory Mac-Leod. Attention. You have three minutes to abandon ship."

Abandon ship! David felt cold fear clutch at his heart. What were they going to do? Three minutes. He had to find Adam. He dashed to the open engine-room door and started down.

Outside he heard Rory's voice, tight with controlled anger. "Who the devil are you to tell me to abandon my own ship." The voice crackled through a megaphone.

"Ahoy, *Island Phantom*," repeated the calm voice from the submarine. "You have less than three minutes to abandon ship. There is a time bomb set to go off aboard your boat."

A time bomb! Someone on board must have set it. It could only be Adam—and where would he set a bomb? Somewhere in the engine room, of course.

David ran down the steel steps until he could peer below the level of the deck. Gleaming machinery everywhere, but no sign of Adam.

Then Rory's voice again, strained, angry. "All hands on deck. Now. Prepare to abandon ship."

He had to do it, of course, David thought. What choice had he? Abandon the *Phantom*. David could imagine the cold fury Rory must be feeling. Impotent fury.

He went down to take a look around. He knew nothing about the engine room and his chance of finding the time bomb was remote. Nevertheless he went, taking a firm grip on himself. He had three minutes. Nearly. That was quite a while, really. But could you set a time bomb that accurately? It might take longer. Or shorter.

He turned and started to run up the steps again, then froze in horror. Above him the door to the deck had slammed shut. He heard the dogs being jammed down into place.

"Hey! Wait a minute! I'm down here!" He raced up the ladder in panic, beat on the door with his fists. "Help! Someone! Let me out!"

No answer. He stopped, breathless, and forced himself to listen.

He heard Rory's voice, still from the bridge. "Abandon ship. Never mind the lifeboat—you haven't time. Jump and swim for the submarine. Now. Abandon ship!"

He heard confused voices, then a distant splash. Another. The crew were leaving. Again he beat on the door and called out. No answer.

Then Rory's voice again, still on the megaphone. "Sandy, where are you? Where's David? He was going to find Adam. See that he's not in the engine room."

Thank God. Cold sweat ran down David's back and arms. "I'm in here," he yelled.

"Coming, Davie." It was Sandy. He heard a rush of running feet, then the dogs being turned back. The door was flung open and he leapt into the fresh air.

"That was close," she said, breathless. "Someone must have closed the door without knowing you were down there. Quick, close it again. It might help to contain the blast."

They slammed the door shut—then time ran out. The deck heaved beneath their feet. The door was flung back by a blast of hot air. A roar pounded in their ears.

David was smashed against the opposite bulkhead. Dimly he saw Sandy hit the whaler and fall to the deck. He reached out to her, grabbing for the straps of her life jacket. The deck beneath him suddenly heaved again. The port side reared in the air, tearing him from Sandy and sending him skidding across the deck. Another blast. A great rush of tortured air flung him about like a rag doll.

Ship and sea dropped away, whirling now overhead, now far below. Then the surface was rushing up in a gyrating mass and suddenly the cold water swallowed him down . . . down . . .

7

David was vaguely conscious of green water encasing him, of tortured lungs demanding air. He kicked desperately but it seemed he must go on and on to the bottom. Then, at last, his momentum stopped. The buoyancy of his life jacket began to take effect and finally he shot up.

The surface broke and he was aware only of life-giving air and his need for it. Then consciousness came flooding back. He looked around.

Before him was Black Rock Island, its grim cliffs sweeping out of the sea. He turned full circle. There was no sign of the *Phantom*. Was she gone already, sunk, a shattered hulk?

Where was everybody? Where was the crew that had abandoned ship? Where was Rory, who had probably stayed on his beloved bridge until the ship sank under him? Where was the submarine? Where was Sandy?

Sandy! She had been with him when that second blast had blown him overboard and, he remembered, she had been wearing a life jacket too. There was a good chance...

A long swell gathered its strength beneath him and he suddenly understood why he couldn't see anything. He had been in a deep trough and the approaching sea blocked out all else. Now it lifted him high to its rolling crest and he could see over the green-black waves.

There was the submarine, much farther away than he had expected, and in the fast fading light he could see that men were being hauled from the water to her deck. Good! The crew had survived anyway, and with luck Rory, on the bridge, had been high enough above the explosion to have escaped a direct blast.

But Sandy, where was she? He must find her first before swimming for the submarine and safety.

A few moments later he saw her. At first she was just another part of the wreckage floating in the oil slick that was the *Phantom's* fleeting headstone, but when she moved he recognized her.

"Sandy!" He struck out for her but she disappeared momentarily behind a climbing green wall. Then he was lifted once more by the rolling sea and he spotted her again.

"Sandy!" She didn't seem to hear him. He fought his way over to her.

Oil smeared her face. Shock glazed her eyes. She was swimming mechanically, going nowhere.

"Sandy!" David grabbed her life jacket, shook her, yelled at her. No response. She only stared at him.

Then suddenly there were tears in her eyes. She reached out for him and he caught her as she sobbed in his arms. The cold spray stung their faces and the waves tossed them effortlessly while they clung together.

"Davie," Sandy managed at last, desperately. "What happened?"

"The bomb," he said. "The time bomb in the engine room, remember? Adam must have set it. You were right about him. It was in the engine room and I was locked in down there." He shivered remembering it. "But you came and let me out and then the bomb went off."

"Yes, I remember." She pushed away from him and stared around wildly. "The *Phantom*. Where is she, Davie? Where's Uncle Rory?"

"The *Phantom's* gone," he said, trying to say it gently, "but I think Rory must be all right. I expect he's on the submarine by now. We have to get to the sub too. We'll have to wave so they can see us."

"Do we have to? They sank the *Phantom*."

"We have to, Sandy. It's either that or swim around here for the rest of our lives—which might not be very long. Where is it? Do you see it?"

A swell lifted them and threatened to drag them apart. David twined his hand in the straps of Sandy's preserver and looked around. There was Black Rock Island, its shadowed cliffs frowning down on them. But where was the sub? She should be over there, shouldn't she?

"There," said Sandy, pointing. "Isn't that it?"

Before David could see what she was pointing at the heaving sea dropped them into another deep trough, blotting out everything else. Spume torn from its ragged crest rained down on them.

A moment later they were lifted again. The submarine was there, a grey shape in the gathering dusk.

"She's coming this way," said Sandy. "They must have seen us."

"No. No, I don't think so." David's voice was tense. "She's going the other way, Sandy. Wave! Shout! We mustn't let them leave us."

He let her go so that he too could wave his arms, but the lurking sea caught her away in an instant and he had to go after her. For precious moments he tried to reach her as she fought to get back to him, while the submarine slid ever farther away from them. Finally clinging to each other again, they watched in dread as the submarine receded and merged with the gloom.

"She won't see us now." Sandy said it calmly, and somehow David was almost glad.

"Now what do we do?" she asked quietly.

He didn't answer for a moment. He looked around at the black expanse of restless ocean, broken only by the shadowy ramparts of the hostile fortress, Sgeir Dubh, and was aware of a sickening, lonely fear as the empty wastes of water threatened to overpower them.

David took a long, deep breath and expelled it slowly. Thank God Sandy was there. Oil coated her hair and face, and he saw something like anger in her eyes, but there was no more fear or shock there. She was calm now. She caught his eye and smiled.

"Aren't you glad you put that life jacket on? I'm glad I did. I haven't worn one in years."

He nodded. The jackets would keep them

afloat indefinitely, if the spume didn't drown them and if the water temperature remained bearable.

And if Ramshaw had received his message by now, David thought, the *Audax* might already be steaming full speed for Black Rock Island. On the other hand, darkness was fast enveloping their watery world.

"We'll just have to hang on until the destroyer gets here."

"Perhaps we could reach the island."

"Don't forget that's where the submarine is. Now that they've gone I'm not sure I want to be rescued by that lot. Not if there's another way. Is there any other landing place besides the channel you were talking about?"

"Not that I know of. It's very unlikely."

Endlessly the sea rolled beneath them, lifting them easily. Each crest split in a long slash that spilled forth gleaming pearls of phosphorescent water, then rolled on, dropping them into a deepening furrow as another swell gathered itself beneath them. Stinging spray whipped into their faces. It grew dark except for a faint light overhead where the moon was trying to pierce the tattered clouds.

Sandy roused herself and dashed the water from her eyes. "We'll be too far away from the island by morning."

David looked around. "Where is it?"

"Somewhere to the south." She had to shout as the wind snatched the words from her lips. "Can you find the North Star?"

But the stars were hidden behind scudding cloud. The island was lost in darkness.

"Which way is the sea taking us?"

"East, I think. Unless the wind has changed."

At least, thought David, they were not being carried out into the endless Atlantic. "The Navy will find us if only we can hang on until morning."

Briefly the moon shone through a thin patch of cloud and in the light the crests gleamed and the troughs were black and rolling. The waves climbed higher, tossing David and Sandy to incredible heights, then curled over and slapped them in the face before dropping them sickeningly back into the depths.

They clung to each other, terrified of being torn apart, letting the water have its way with them. If they could just last until dawn...

"We'll make it," said Sandy suddenly, confidently. The sea was endless and contemptuous of them in its might, but suddenly David felt sure she was right.

They lost all awareness of time. They knew only the waves and the lashing spray, the choking water and the taste of salt, the gulps of precious air and the comforting presence of each other. Together they waited for the light.

When it seemed that dawn would never come, Sandy suddenly looked up and David felt her stiffen. In a lull in the crying gale a new sound came to them.

"Davie!" Sandy shouted. "Listen!"

He dashed the water from his ears and listened

into the wind. Sure enough he heard it, a sound that might have been there a long time but that was now growing louder: a dull, booming reverberation.

"What is it?" he yelled.

"Surf. Waves pounding on cliffs. The sea must be carrying us toSgeir Dubh."

David peered vainly into the murk. Spume lashed into his face and he had to turn away from it. The black sea swept away from under them again, dropping them deep. He clutched desperately at Sandy's jacket.

Another swell tore at them, lifting them. For a moment they were borne aloft where a faint light far overhead outlined the steep cliffs. They could see where the seas beat relentlessly against the base of the island, flinging spray up the black ramparts.

Cold dread gripped David. In a few moments the waves would gather them up and hurl them against the towering rocks.

"Sandy! We've got to get away. Let's swim for it."

But she shook her head and clung to him. Spray from the pounding surf fell on them like torrential rain. A sliver of light from the moon showed them the walls of rock towering over them like an enormous gravestone. Then a great wave lifted them and swept them with terrible speed at the black mass.

At the last moment the wave flattened out and dropped them into a shallow trough where the beaten seas gathered their forces for a new assault. Suddenly the moon came out and cast a faint light over the scene. It danced on the showering spray and lay yellow across the scarred cliffs. David gripped Sandy in sudden hope, for a pale shaft of moonlight had picked out a deep, narrow shadow in the face of the cliff.

"Sandy!" he cried. "A cave! Swim for it!"

She turned to look and the backwash of the wave tore her away from him. He reached desperately for her but he was too late. She vanished.

"Sandy!" he cried again, battling against the might of the surf. "Sandy!" The sea pounded in his ears, over his head, smothering him in a welter of foam. When he fought out of it the moon was gone, leaving the world black and wild and madly alive. The next swell caught him and hurled him forward.

He awaited the crushing blow that must follow, his arms upraised despairingly.

8

The crashing surf pounded the rocks, almost drowning out the wild moaning of the wind. Black Rock Island stood alone over the grey ocean vastness, a vastness that seemed to have swallowed the *Phantom* totally, betraying no sign that she had ever existed.

David regained consciousness slowly. For a moment he feared he must still be out there, adrift in the black, rolling sea, but he felt solid rock beneath him and his fear abated.

Then it surged back like a tidal wave, overwhelming him with its enormity. *Sandy!* In his mind's eye he remembered her being torn away from him by the crashing waves, losing sight of her entirely as the surf catapulted him towards the island. Then blackness, nothing.

He moaned and opened his eyes.

In the dim light he saw only a tall, narrow triangle that framed angry seas and scudding clouds. He began to look around carefully, every movement causing his muscles to ache. He was in a cave—a shallow one, he guessed, for the grey light penetrated to a wall of rock behind him. But on either side dark shadows hung, obscuring everything else within.

David sat up but had to hang onto his head for a minute as the cave seemed to float into the air and roll over. When it returned to normal he was suddenly aware of Sandy sitting beside him, looking at him anxiously.

"Davie! Are you all right?"

"Sandy! Thank God!" He reached out and hugged her to him. "I thought you hadn't made it," he choked out.

"I was afraid *you* weren't going to," she replied, releasing herself from his grip. "You really had me worried."

He looked down at himself. His pants and sleeves were torn in places but his sneakers were still on his feet. And his life jacket was still fastened about him. Another, he realized, was folded under his head. Sandy's.

"Thanks for the pillow," he grinned. "How about you, Sandy? Are you okay?"

"About the same as you, I suppose, with a sore ankle as well. Slightly sprained, I think."

"Oh-oh. Let's see it."

She sat down carefully, wincing, and thrust out her bare foot. He cupped her heel gently in his hand. The ankle was swollen and slightly discoloured. "Hurt much?"

She shook her head. "Not if I stay off it. And I shouldn't have any problem doing that. There's no place to go."

"We could explore the cave a little and see if there's any way out—though I doubt it. What time do you suppose it is anyway?"

"Judging by the position of the sun it's late afternoon."

"Late afternoon! Are you sure?" He looked out over the heaving water. "I hope we haven't missed sighting a search party!"

She shook her head. "I don't suppose we'd see one if it did come down here. Let me show you." She struggled to her feet, using him as a crutch to hobble to the cave mouth.

Before them a shelf of rock sloped to the water. Beyond it the seas rolled in to break in a smother of foam over an unseen barrier. The spent waves curled on up over the slope to the cave, but only the wind-driven spray reached them. On the left the shelf tapered off to merge with the cliffs and on the right it ended abruptly against a wall of rock that jutted out at right angles.

"You see," said Sandy, "we're at the northern end of the island but we're facing west. You can catch a glimpse of St. Kilda away over there when the overcast lifts. The entrance to the lochan is on the east side, so if a ship came down from the north and went directly to the channel she wouldn't pass this way at all."

David looked around anxiously. On either side of the cave the surf pounded savagely. Overhead the cliff was sheer, unbroken. There was no escape.

"Well, it looks as if we haven't much choice about what we do next. But I don't think we need to worry. The Navy will be looking all around this area and there must be others who will miss the *Phantom* before long."

But she shook her head. "We can't count on that, Davie. Not for days. Some people knew we were going from Leverburgh to Barra, of course, but we seldom keep a strict schedule. Usually on that run we go through the straits and down the east coast of the Long Island. If anyone saw us coming this way they'd likely think we were going out to St. Kilda. And then possibly somewhere else. Eventually when we don't show up everybody will be looking for us, but that could be three or four days from now."

David whistled soundlessly through his teeth, his brow furrowed. "And I suppose those guys on the submarine know all that. Adam would at least. Still it seems to me they took quite a risk in sinking the *Phantom*."

"I can't believe it," said Sandy fiercely. "The *Phantom* gone. After all these years, after surviving the war. And now being sunk by a bunch of smugglers." David could see tears in her eyes. "Adam. I never really liked him but I can hardly believe he would do that. He must have been one of them all the time—maybe even the driver who hit our engineer. That means he's a—a murderer. And maybe he killed that man you found at the foot of the cliff too, pushed him over from the top, then ran down to 'discover' him. He could even have killed Uncle Rory and the crew with that bomb. And you and me too."

"In fact," said David slowly, "he probably thinks he did just that."

"You're right!" Her eyes widened. "We're missing, aren't we? They probably think we're dead."

She clung to him and her fingers bit into his arm. "Oh, Davie, Uncle Rory will think so too. It'll break his heart. If he has a chance, he'll kill Adam." Her voice trembled.

"They won't give him a chance, you can be sure of that. I'm just trying to figure out what they're doing. They took a big chance in sinking the *Phantom* and now they're saddled with prisoners. In a few days they'll have roused a regular hornets' nest when people realize that Rory and the *Phantom* are missing. So even if they know nothing about Ramshaw and the *Audax* they're playing with fire. There's only one explanation."

"What's that?"

"That they're about to close up their base here and move on. Perhaps they were smuggling arms into Ireland or something. In fact, come to think of it, Ramshaw did say he had reason to believe that it would be all over in a week or two at the most. I wonder how much he *does* know. Anyway, my guess is they've just about finished whatever they're doing here and can't take chances on anyone butting in now."

"Davie," she said suddenly, fiercely, "we've got to stop them. We can't let them get away. Not after what they've done. Not if they're smuggling arms or drugs or that kind of thing. We've *got* to stop them. No one else can!"

He shook his head reluctantly. "What can we do? I'm still counting on Ramshaw and his destroyer. He'll have my message by now, or will have soon if he isn't back from London yet. Then

I'm sure he'll send the ship down here right away."

"But we can't count on that." She frowned up at the cliffs looming overhead and on both sides. He knew what she was looking for.

"We'll never climb those, Sandy." He too scanned the bare rock face, the restless sea and the narrow ledge on which they stood. The cave must be practically invisible from out there, he thought. Even from close in it would just look like a triangular shadow in the scarred battlements.

"Sandy" he said suddenly, marvelling, "do you know how lucky we were to be washed up right here at this one safe spot?"

"Lucky? Luck has nothing to do with it. It wasn't just luck that I put on a life jacket for the first time in years. Or that we ended up here, as you say. Oh, no. 'All things work together for good to those who love God.' The question is, why were we brought here if there's no way we can get away again? It doesn't make sense."

He nodded. He was thinking of one narrow shelf of rock and one cave, a tiny slit in an entire cliff; of surly seas threatening to smash them and instead depositing them at this one and only refuge.

"It's hard to believe," he said finally. "I wouldn't be surprised if we're the only ones who've ever been in this cave, the only ones who know it exists."

"There you're wrong," Sandy said, a sparkle suddenly lighting her eyes.

"Wrong? How?"

"Come with me and I'll show you. Before you woke up I had a look around."

She picked up her life jacket, shrugged into it, and using the beam from its little emergency light, hobbled to one shadowy side of the cave. At the back corner was another fissure in the rock. They edged into it, through it, and found themselves in another room where the roof was so close above their heads they had to crouch.

Sandy put her hand on David's arm, stopping him. "Are you thirsty?"

"Thirsty? Don't mention it. I've been trying not to think about it."

"Listen."

He obliged, curious. At first he heard only the muffled booming of the surf and the wail of the wind beyond the walls. But then he heard something else: a steady *drip . . . drip . . . drip.*

"It's water. Fresh water. Look." She moved her light so that it shone on the rock beside them. Water was running down the wall. And just above the floor, where the wall cut back, it fell free into a cleft in the floor that carried it away into the shadows.

He tasted it and sighed with relief. "Lovely! Fresh water. That's a load off my mind. What more can we ask?"

"Tea!" said Sandy promptly. "A cup of hot tea and a bowl of hot porridge. Now come and see what else I found." There was a mixture of mystery and triumph in her voice. "Look at this."

A ring of stones, blackened on the inside, was arranged on the floor of the cave—apparently an old fireplace.

"Well, what do you know!" Kneeling to examine them, David found pieces of charred wood inside the ring beneath a coating of ashes and dust.

"And that's not all. There's a big pot over there." Sandy pointed it out. "It's as old as the hills. Rusty, but still sound."

"Sandy," he said slowly, "do you know what I'm beginning to think?"

"Yes, I know," she replied. "You're thinking we've found Conuil's Cave."

He grinned at her. "Have we?"

"Yes, I'm sure of it. Wait till Uncle Rory sees this. He'll be green with envy to think that a Canadian should see it before he does."

"I don't blame him; it's hardly fair. Tell me the story again—all the details."

She sat on the cold floor beside him. "The Conuil brothers were in trouble with Cumberland's troops for hiding Prince Charlie. In their flight they came to Black Rock Island. The soldiers followed them here and searched the island but could find no trace of them."

"No wonder," said David, "if they were in here."

"But that's not the end of it, remember. When the troops were sailing away they looked back and saw the Conuils on the cliff top, so they came back and made another search—with the same result. How could the Conuils have got from here to the cliff top?"

"They couldn't. Even with a boat—and a small enough one to hide in the cave—they couldn't have got around to the far side of the island in the time it took the soldiers to set sail again. That part of the story must be fiction."

"Perhaps." But Sandy was obviously not convinced. She sat brooding for a long time. David watched her puzzled face in the dim light, waiting.

"Davie," she said suddenly, "why wouldn't they have been suffocated when they lit a fire in here?"

That took him by surprise. He shook his head. "I don't know. The smoke would have to go out the opening to the outer cave. But it would fill this part first."

"Yes. Unless there's a chimney here."

"A chimney? Are you serious?"

"Yes. A natural chimney, I mean. It's possible." Suddenly she unfastened the little light from her jacket and used it to examine the roof. Above the ring of blackened stones the inner cave was only about waist-high. Crouched low, David moved gingerly over the stones, exploring the rock above with his fingers.

"There *is* a cleft here." He felt a spark of excitement. "It's quite wide too. But surely you don't think—"

"That it goes right up to the cliff top? Why not?" She crawled over beside him. "There! Did you feel that?" In the dim light her eyes were sparkling. "There's fresh air coming down. It *must* go right up."

He looked up into the blackness of the cleft. For a long minute he saw nothing, then far overhead something moved and he could make out a sliver of daylight.

"You're right. It is a natural chimney."

"And a big one, isn't it?"

"Sure is. Wide enough for Santa Claus to come down, this end anyway."

"Or," she slowly, "for the Conuils to go up."

He looked at her, startled. "You're kidding!"

"You," she accused, "are a doubting Thomas. Move over and let me in there."

He scrunched aside and she moved under the cleft, then stood up. Her head and shoulders disappeared.

"Move over here," she said, her voice muffled but excited, "so I can stand on you."

He cupped her foot and lifted. She put her weight on his shoulders momentarily, then she was gone. After a moment's silence there was a sudden "Ouch!" and her foot was groping for him again. He caught it and guided her down. She crouched beside him, her eyes dancing.

"It's true, Davie! It's not only a chimney, it's a staircase as well. *That's* how the Conuils were able to get back up to the top of the cliff."

"Let me see." He ducked inside the cleft and stood up. His hands moved over the cold rock surface.

All at once his doubts vanished. They were there all right. Handholds, footholds—shallow, irregular niches hacked out of solid rock. He groped for them and pulled himself up until his feet were inside the chimney. His toes found the lowest step. He reached up farther. Yes, there were more of them. He lowered himself back to the floor of the cave.

"I'd never have believed it! That must have

been some job cutting all those niches in the rock face clear to the top—if they really go that far. How long were the Conuils here anyway?"

"Not long enough to do all that. At least, not as far as I know. They must have been here before, of course. Maybe they even lived here at one time, or someone else did. What a perfect hiding place in time of clan wars."

They crouched there in the ring of stones. A black streak across Sandy's nose gave her an impish look. David grinned at her. "I've got to hand it to you, Sandy. I never would have thought of looking for a staircase to the cliff top."

She nodded modestly. "It was brilliant." She laughed. "Or more likely plain stubbornness. I wasn't going to admit that any part of the Conuil story was just fable. And I couldn't believe we'd been brought this far only to rot in a cave. So"— she rubbed her chin and left another black smudge—"now we can follow their example and get up there and find out what's going on."

"Right. And the sooner the better. It won't be too long before dark and I want to find out whether or not the *Audax* has been here."

"Then you'd better go ahead. It's going to take me a long time to climb up there with my ankle."

"Oh, I'm sorry, I forgot about your ankle. That will be a tough climb and there's not much I can do to help. Unless I could come behind and help to take your weight?"

"No, that would take too long. You go on ahead before it gets dark. By the time you've had a look around I should be up there. But you'll have to be careful. The smugglers may be somewhere around, and there's the terrain itself to watch out for."

"What's it like up there?"

"The surface is rocks and heather. But you'll have to mind the clefts—if there's one as deep as this one there may be others. The loch is down near the other end of the island, surrounded by hills. The cave Uncle Rory and I found is in the side of a hill above the loch—the west side. It's about halfway up and the opening is covered by bushes so it's almost impossible to see until you're right there. The highest point is above and to the left of the cave when you're facing it. Uncle Rory and I named it Lookout Peak. Not one of our better efforts, I suppose, but you can see a long way from there."

"Right. That may be the place to head for if nothing's going on anywhere else."

"But you'll have to be awfully careful. There will likely be a lookout at the peak or someone on watch at the cave."

"Don't worry. I'll be careful. If anyone's there I'll see him before he sees me."

He suddenly caught her hand, squeezed it and grinned at her. "See you up top. Soon." Then he vanished into the cleft.

Most of the handholds on the long climb to the top were mere nicks. Soon David's fingers and toes ached from the effort. Now and then he came upon wide, smooth ledges with plenty of room to rest his feet as he straddled the chimney. He paused there to catch his breath and to thank the unknowns who, many years ago, had carved the ledges for their own use.

The air became increasingly fresh. He could feel the coolness of it on his face. Then his groping fingers found the rim of the chimney and caught the wiry stems of the overhanging heather. He pushed the plants aside, pulled himself from the cleft and lay panting on the ground.

In a minute he was up again, sprinting for the rise ahead of him. At the top of it he looked back. It was understandable why the cave had never been discovered from above. Anyone searching the island from the south would almost certainly stop here. Before him lay only a small triangle of ground, not more than a stone's throw to the apex. The other two sides of the triangle were cliff edges marking sheer drops to the sea far below. The ground itself was rocky, covered here and there with ragged heather. No one would suspect the existence of an opening to a cave at the bottom of the cliff.

David headed south. The surface of the island seemed to be made up of a series of slopes and valleys running roughly east and west in a crescent curve. To the south he could see a hilltop dominating the island. Lookout Peak, he surmised. He lay down and watched it carefully for several minutes but saw no sign of activity. Reassured, he moved in the general direction of the peak. He crossed three ridges; at the top of the fourth he crouched in the heather and gazed below.

He was looking down into a deep valley. A long way below him the wind-plucked waters of a tiny loch spread across the basin, the hills around it almost forming a cup. There was no sign of either the submarine or the *Audax*. There was nothing. The place was empty.

A worried frown creased David's brow. Had the destroyer been here or not? Where was the submarine and her crew? Where were the crew of the *Phantom?* He'd have to head for the cave to find out, he decided. He stood up and started down the hill.

A sudden voice came from behind him. "Put up your hands and turn around."

David froze. His heart sank. Slowly he raised his hands above his head and turned. He was looking into the black muzzle of a rifle.

9

It was a moment before David realized that the man behind the gun was Adam Brieve.

Adam was staring at him in frank astonishment. "Where the hell," he finally said, "did you come from?"

That, David determined, Adam must never know. He gestured in the general direction of the eastern cliff. "Out there."

"Obviously." Adam's dark eyes glinted. "Where did you come ashore then?"

David was going to lower his arms but thought better of it and nodded towards the loch. "Down there, I guess."

"You *guess?* What's that mean? Am I supposed to believe you swam all the way here from where the *Phantom* went down?"

"I don't really know what happened." David hoped Adam would accept that. "I vaguely remember being in the water for what seemed like ages, then washing through some kind of opening in the cliff and ending up on shore. Next thing I know I'm wandering around in the hills. I just don't know." He tried to sound hopelessly confused.

Adam was still staring at him, shaking his head in disbelief. "You must be right," he said, "unless you're a human fly. You're the luckiest man alive, I can tell you that much."

"What's going on anyway?" David continued. "Where are Rory and Sandy and the rest of the crew?"

"They're all right," grunted Adam. "They're in a cave down there on the hillside, all except the girl. Don't know what happened to her."

David was shocked at Adam's blunt tone. "You mean she's lost?"

"Yeah. Too bad she wasn't in the habit of wearing a life jacket," Adam sneered. He moved the muzzle of the gun against David's back. "Over this way," he ordered, steering him towards the eastern cliff.

"What are you going to do with us?"

"I don't know about you." Adam sounded just a little amused. "We decided to keep Rory and the crew alive for a while to help load the sub when we leave here for good. But five extra people is just about our limit; you're going to be a nuisance. Maybe we'll let you go and use you for target practice when the crew of the sub is looking for relaxation."

David could hardly believe Adam's callousness. Where the blazes was the *Audax?* What had gone wrong with his message to Ramshaw? What could he do about Sandy? If only he could get away . . .

"Look, Adam," he said, steadying his voice,

"what's going on anyway? What are you smuggling?"

"Anything that's profitable," said Adam carelessly. "We're not specialists." He eased the pressure of the rifle against David's back. They were almost at the top of the cliff.

"Stop here," he said. "Sit right there with your hands in front of you where I can see them." His own arm cradled the rifle and his eyes never left David.

"I knew you got something from Johnny Cairns," he continued conversationally. "It was obvious—the cut boot lace. And of course I found the map when you carelessly left it in your coat pocket in the hotel."

He's proud of himself, thought David. Cocky because he's got the upper hand. Maybe if I can keep him talking...

"Is that why you got me onto the *Phantom,* so you could keep an eye on me in case he had told me something?"

"That's right. I was already there to watch Rory in case he got too interested in this island, so one more didn't matter. Two birds with one stone. Or one time bomb.

"You fools! I overheard you planning to come down here and see how the birds were acting, so all we had to do was set prearranged plans into motion. It was too bad about the *Phantom* though. She was a tidy little ship." He sounded genuinely sorry.

"You can't expect to get away with it." David hoped he sounded more convincing than he felt.

"Everybody will be looking for the *Phantom* by now. Everybody knows Rory; they'll miss him."

But Adam shook his head and waved his free hand towards the grey sea. "Do you see anyone out there looking for him? No. And you won't for three or four days. By then we'll be long gone, sitting under a palm tree being fanned by native girls." He grinned in anticipation. "Besides, the first trace of the *Phantom* will be found well south of here and that's where the search will concentrate."

"What do you mean? What trace?"

"Oh, bits of wreckage, a life jacket with her name on it. Things like that. The sub picked them up after the ship went down. She's unloading them somewhere to keep the search away from this area. Just to be on the safe side. We're thorough."

They were that, thought David grimly. But there was still the *Audax* and Ramshaw. What on earth were they doing?

It was uncanny, as if Adam had read his thoughts. "You can forget about that destroyer up at Stornoway too. She's still berthed there at the jetty without the slightest idea what's going on."

"But—" David caught himself before he said the Laird's name. He need not have bothered.

"Ramshaw?" Adam chuckled. "You can forget about him too."

Suddenly David's last hope faded. They knew. And if they hadn't known before, it was he himself who had given the Laird away because his gull's feather had drawn Ramshaw's attention on board the *Skerryvore*.

I've got to do something, he thought, and soon. But I've got a gun pointed at me. Maybe with a little more time . . .

"Have you been smuggling arms to Ireland?" he asked.

"Among other things. With all the terrorist movements in the world today there's plenty of profit in arms. Enough to keep the submarine and the *Storvik* on the hop."

"The *Storvik?*" David remembered clearly the trawler that had crossed their path after the *Phantom* had left Tobermory. A Swedish trawler, Rory had said, that hadn't left with the herring fleets because of an accidental grounding.

"Yes, she's one of us. But we won't be needing her anymore. Or the submarine for that matter."

"You mean you're giving up the—the trade?"

"That's right." Adam sounded smugly satisfied. "We're on the brink of the biggest haul we've ever made. When you're a millionaire there's no point in continuing to risk your neck."

"A millionaire! I had no idea there was that much money in weapons."

"There isn't usually, not for us deck hands. But *this* is something else."

"What on earth are you selling then? Tanks?"

"Snoopy, aren't you?" Adam growled. "But you won't be around to tell anyone anyway." He chuckled and it was not a pleasant sound. "Not tanks. Something a lot more effective than tanks. And easier to handle."

David felt a growing uneasiness in the pit of his stomach. "What are you talking about?"

"Ever heard of germ warfare?"

David's uneasiness threatened to overwhelm him. "Of course," he said softly.

"Well, someone's isolated a—what do you call it?—a bacillus, a kind of germ. Anthrax. And not just ordinary anthrax either. A new strain that will wipe out a country's cattle population like *that*." He snapped his fingers. "And of course," he added slowly, "it's fatal to humans who come into contact with the cows."

David turned and stared at Adam in horror. "And you're selling *that* to terrorists?"

"Not quite yet," said Adam. "Soon. MI5 found out about the stuff and confiscated it in a rather spectacular raid and right now it's heavily guarded in a secret chamber near London. But the boss is about to get his hands on enough of it to put us all on easy street."

David stared at him in sick disbelief. Not that kind of deadly bacillus in the hands of terrorists! More than ever now he had to do something. Anything. If it wasn't already too late.

"What—what are you still waiting around for then?"

"We're not waiting much longer. It's just about over. The sub is picking up the boss and the stuff tonight and coming back here for us the day after tomorrow. Then we'll all be heading for some South Sea paradise."

"What makes you think they'll come back for you?"

"Oh, they'll be back. Tonight the *Storvik's* dropping off some of the boss's personal things— family valuables or something—before she docks at Tarbert to pick up the rest of our lads. I don't know why he bothers—he'll be able to buy anything he wants after this haul. But you don't argue with the boss. Anyway, it's our insurance that he'll come back here."

David's mind was racing. He had to get away somehow, had to tell Ramshaw about their plans. No more time to waste.

He had been facing Adam; now he looked out over the cliff to the sea. "That looks like the *Storvik* coming now," he said casually.

"Where?"

The muzzle never wavered from its fix on David. And yet for just that one moment, he told himself, Adam's attention must slacken. He leapt up and brought his arm down hard, knocking the rifle aside just as it went off with a roar. Adam lurched backwards, trying to bring the rifle back to bear, but David was on him, grabbing at his throat. As Adam tried to move away David suddenly shoved him back, making him drop the weapon. Desperately David grabbed for it but Adam was onto him before he could turn it. David thrust upward with the barrel and Adam fell away, cursing, clutching his head.

David stood, his hands trembling, his breath coming in gasps, the gun trained on Adam.

"You stupid bloody fool!" Brieve's face was livid, his eyes blazing. "What good is that going to do you? Where are you going now?"

"I'm not going to let you get away with it,"

David panted. "Not without fighting back. You won't have it all your way now."

Adam laughed through his fury. "Come on, McCrimmon, don't make matters worse for yourself. Give me back the gun and come down to the cave like a good boy. If you don't, believe me you'll be hunted down like a dog and shot. There's nowhere you can go and in a while there'll be the whole crew of the trawler scouting every part of this island."

He's right, thought David, except for one thing. He doesn't know about the cave at the foot of the cliff. History was going to be repeating itself—a search for an escaped prisoner across the hills of Black Rock Island, and the prisoner's unexplained disappearance.

"Go with you and wait to be disposed of?" he scoffed. "No thanks. I'll take my chances out here." He backed away slowly, the gun still pointing at Adam, then turned and ran westward.

At the top of the first hill he stopped to look back. There was no sign of anyone. The valley was empty.

Reassured, he turned northward towards the cave and Sandy. He found her without any trouble, lying in the heather near the top of the cleft.

"What happened?" she demanded as David came up beside her. "I heard a shot."

"It's all right, but we need to stay near the cave now." He led her to the top of the nearest ridge, where they could watch for any sign of Adam, then told her everything he had found out.

Sandy looked at him thoughtfully when he had finished. "There's only one thing to do,

Davie," she said slowly. "You're going to have to get yourself recaptured."

For a moment the full meaning of what she'd said didn't sink in. Then David stared at her. "What? Sandy, for heaven's sake! You don't know what you're saying!"

"Yes, I do," she said heavily. "I'm awfully sorry. I wish there was some other way, but there isn't." She caught his hand and held it. "Think about it. Adam said that the *Storvik* was coming here tonight with the boss's valuables or something, didn't he? And that she'd be going back to Tarbert? That's a God-given opportunity to get away from here and get help. One of us has to be on her when she sails."

He shook his head, puzzled. "We'd never make it. They'll be looking all over the island for me. We'd never get *near* the trawler."

"Not *we,* David. Me. That's why you have to get caught again. They have no idea I'm here at all, right? So as soon as they have you they'll call off the hunt. By then it'll be dark and I should have no trouble stowing away."

He had to admit that she had a point but he shook his head, rebelling. There had to be some other way. After risking his life to get away it was just too much to ask him to go back. No telling what Adam would do to him, whether he'd even be left alive long enough for Sandy to get help.

"I just don't know if I can do it, Sandy. And you'd be taking an awful risk."

"We both have to take risks, David. Have you any idea what that bacillus could do? Ordinary anthrax is bad enough. I remember one farmer

118

who had to destroy his whole herd because one of his cows *might* have it. They couldn't take the chance. And according to Adam this is an even deadlier strain, one fatal to people. If terrorists get hold of that they can bargain for anything. It would be like holding a gun to the head of the whole world. We *have* to take the chance."

"But after what I did to Adam and what I know now," David said, "how am I going to get recaptured without getting killed? What if Adam decides to shoot first and ask questions later?"

"That I don't know. Somehow you'll have to let them discover you, and you're going to have to be awfully convincing. I know what I'm asking, Davie, and I'm praying you won't get hurt. But it's the only way I can see."

"Where's this place, Tarbert?" he asked, delaying the decision. "What will you do when you get there?"

"Tarbert's in Harris, not too far from Scalpay where the *Storvik* grounded. There's a hotel there. I can telephone Ramshaw or the police for help. There's a good road to Stornoway too. But I have to get there first."

It was true. If she could escape she'd be able to do something—which was more than they could do stuck on Black Rock Island. And, he admitted, facing up to it, she'd have no chance of escaping as long as he was at large.

"I wish to heaven you were wrong," he said, "but I'm very much afraid you're right."

"I'm sorry." She squeezed his hand. "I wish we could both go on the *Storvik*." She cheered a little with a new thought. "You'll be with Uncle

Rory. At least you can tell him what's going on and that I'm really alive and kicking."

David nodded. "If I make it back to the cave in one piece maybe we'll have a chance to do something too before this is all over. There'll be six of us and I doubt there's that many of them, at least not when the sub and trawler aren't here."

Her voice was anxious again. "Don't take any more chances than you have to, Davie. Please. Going back there is dangerous enough. Leave it up to Ramshaw and the Navy."

"I can't think of anything we could do anyway, but you never know. Well"—reluctantly he began to rise—"if I'm going I'd better go now before the island is crawling with trigger-happy smugglers." She was still holding his hand and he reached over to touch her face. "Be careful, Sandy. It would come as quite a shock to some people, but I'll be praying for you."

She grinned. "Promise? And I for you so we've nothing to worry about."

He stood up and walked cautiously southward. Before long he was looking down into the valley where the lochan lay. At first he saw no one. Then he became aware of two men, one of them Adam, crouched together near the spot where he had been caught earlier. They seemed to be lying in wait for something. Both were armed with rifles.

David dropped to his belly and wriggled forward through the heather to a low area between two rises. It seemed hours before he decided he was close enough to the men. They were just over

120

the larger rise in front of him, partly hidden by mounds of grass and heather.

Slowly, feeling painfully vulnerable, David turned so he was facing away from the men. He raised Adam's rifle and pointed it over the knoll that was now before him.

Then, very deliberately, all the while expecting to hear the whine of a bullet heading for his back, he sneezed.

The men whirled around, their rifles coming up sharply. "Freeze!" ordered Adam, training his gun squarely on David.

He turned and raised his hands high above his head, dropping the rifle. He had no trouble appearing scared to death. For one terrible moment he thought they were going to shoot anyway. Then they relaxed, although they still trained their rifles on him.

Adam, his head bandaged, spoke first. "Too bad you're such a miserable quarry," he snarled. "I was looking forward to several enjoyable hours of hunting you down. Just don't cause us any more problems, McCrimmon, or your life is going to end right now. Behave yourself and we'll let you have a few extra hours."

David dropped his hands and headed down the hill towards the cave.

10

The loch was empty. No sign of the trawler yet, but Sandy was ready for her. Thanks to David's sacrifice she had been able to observe the island and its occupants all evening from a peak overlooking the loch. As darkness settled in she had her route down to the water's edge and the location of the four smugglers she had been able to catch glimpses of etched clearly in her mind's eye.

One of the men was on Lookout Peak making regular sweeps of the surrounding seascape through a pair of binoculars. The other three were in the cave where the prisoners, now including David, were being held. Unless there were more of them that she hadn't spotted they shouldn't give her any trouble.

She scraped up some loose earth and rubbed it over her face and hands, then in the moonless darkness lowered herself over the first precipitous ridge. For a moment she went sliding down steep bare rock. Something dislodged beneath her feet and rattled down the hillside. Then the bluff levelled out and she lay still for a moment, listening. There was only the wind whistling across the hills and the distant *boom* of the sea against the cliffs.

Reassured, she went on down the long slope until the incline tapered off. She paused again, searching until she saw some black shapes huddled along the shoreline. Rocks. In a moment there was one more black shape crouched there, waiting.

She had no idea how much time passed before there was movement in the vicinity of the cave. First a light showed briefly, then two men came down the hill toward the loch, every now and then flashing the light to pick out their path.

At the water's edge the men busied themselves for a moment with something at their feet, then pushed a small dinghy into the loch. One of them jumped into it and began to row out into the darkness. Sandy could mark his progress only by the thin beam of his flashlight rising and falling with the waves.

At last the reason for his action became apparent. Well out into the darkness the man suddenly turned a bright light onto what seemed a solid wall of rock. Then came an answering light, higher up on the wall. A moment later the *Storvik* emerged from the obscure passage that led to the open sea. As her bow swung towards where Sandy crouched, the man in the dinghy climbed aboard.

The trawler came slowly shoreward, her light playing across the surface of the loch. Sandy sank deeper into the welcome shadows of the rocks as the light lifted and swung along the shoreline. The *Storvik* drew in closer until shadowy figures were visible on her deck. Sandy heard the screw churn the water as it spun in reverse, the rattle of the heavy chain and finally a splash. The anchor was down. All was quiet.

It must have been Adam Brieve who had rowed out to guide the *Storvik* through the opening, because she could see him now at the rail. He scrambled down the rope ladder and stepped into the little dinghy that bobbed on the end of a painter. Five blue suitcases were lowered down to him; then he cast loose and rowed the short distance to shore.

Before he was quite there he called out to his companion, "There's five with her tonight, including the skipper. When I've unloaded this stuff the crew's coming up to the cave for a celebration. Go on ahead and crack open some whiskey."

So the ship would be vacated, Sandy decided, relieved. She would have no trouble getting aboard and hiding away for the trip to Tarbert. She just had to wait.

She watched Adam unload the suitcases from the dinghy, then row back out to the trawler. Four men climbed down the ladder to join him in the little boat and once again he made the trip back to shore.

Four men. Sandy frowned. That meant there was still one aboard on anchor watch. It wasn't going to be so easy after all.

The men disappeared in the direction of the

cave. The light on the forecastle went out abruptly. There was sudden silence.

Sandy looked overhead. The moon was rising and the clouds were patchy. It was not going to be as dark as she would have liked.

Her eyes went to the ladder hanging over the side of the trawler. If she could be sure that the crew would stay in the cave and that the lookout on the Peak would be watching the ocean, the ladder was the obvious way to get aboard. But with neither of these conditions guaranteed she thought she had better look elsewhere. For several minutes she crouched there trying to decide what to do.

The clouds disappeared momentarily, revealing the moon and a swath of stars. Their light lay across the restless waters of the loch and backlit the spars and stack of the ship. And it silhouetted the last member of the crew, sitting at the stern. If he's on anchor watch, Sandy thought, he's a long way from the anchor. Oh well, he probably won't stay there long.

But she was wrong. Apparently he was going to have his own celebration. With a bottle for company, which he consulted frequently, he seemed bent on making a night of it.

From her hiding place Sandy could feel the sting of fine spray as the wind buffeted the surface of the loch. It was mounting almost to gale force and the trawler pitched in the waves. But there was no sound from the deck.

The man on watch took a drink from his bottle, then set it down with exaggerated care. He yawned and slumped back against the bulkhead. For a long time he just sat there, his head drooping forward little by little, but he caught himself suddenly and sat up. His groping hands sought the bottle again and he began to sing.

Enough of this, thought Sandy. I'm going to chance it. She squirmed forward out of the shelter of the rocks, scarcely daring to look up. At that moment the man belched loudly, slouched off his seat and disappeared.

Sandy covered the last few steps in a crouch and slipped into the water. She shivered as it groped up her legs and the cold embraced her; then she pushed out into the deep shadow beneath the ship's counter. There was no sound from overhead. Silently she swam around the curve of the stern and looked down the length of the ship. No luck—no ladder on this side.

That left the starboard side, in full view of both the cave and Lookout Peak whenever the moon sailed free of the encumbering clouds. Well, thought Sandy, I'll just have to wait for the darkest possible moment. She made her way to the bow, slipped around it and paused there, a small shadow on the water. Just beyond her the ladder hung down invitingly.

She glanced anxiously overhead. The moon lay beyond patchy cloud but its sheen reached down into the loch, touching the mast, the stack, the ladder. The curving prow cast only a meagre shadow. From it a cable reached down into the depths. The anchor cable! The links were big enough to afford handholds; it was farther from the shore than the ladder and at least partly in deeper gloom. As the darkness deepened just a little Sandy reached for the cable and began to climb. She was out of the water, against the dark hull, pulling herself into the deeper shadow of the prow when disaster stuck.

It must have been seaweed entwined in the chain. Sandy's foot slipped and her sore ankle twisted. Desperately she clutched the cable but her hands slipped too. She fell with a loud *splash.*

Sea water reached her throat. She kicked to the surface, choking. For a moment she was in darkness. Then a bright light beamed out from ashore and fixed her in its glare.

Sandy jerked away, tasting for a split second the bitterness of defeat. I'm not beaten, she thought fiercely. They haven't got me yet.

Suddenly the beam that had caught her in its glare was doused. There was one moment of paralyzed silence, then to Sandy's astonishment a shout of laughter. "Polotski! You bloody fool. No need to watch the anchor that close!"

More laughter, more taunts, then a command. "Get back on board! You won't be relieved for another hour yet."

Get back on board! If that's what they wanted her to do she would certainly oblige. Then she remembered with a shock the real watchman who was somewhere on board, who must surely have heard the shouting. But nothing—no sound from the deck. Had he gone below and not heard anything?

She swam towards the ladder and reached for the bottom rung. Were they still watching from shore? If so, once she was out of the water they would see that she was not the watch, even if they didn't turn the light on again. She looked back over her shoulder in the direction from which the laughter had come but could see nothing, could hear only low voices in conversation.

She climbed quickly until her face came level with the deck. Her shaking hands found the guardrail. No sign of the watch. With an effort she pulled herself up and into the shadows of the superstructure. She crouched and looked anxiously around, listening intently, scarcely able to believe that she'd made it.

A sound came from close at hand. Sandy peered about apprehensively. For a minute she couldn't make it out; then she chuckled in relief at the deep, half-strangled snore that started in the sleeper's boots and bubbled to his mouth in a series of honks and gasps. The watchman lay sprawled on his back, feet and hands flung wide, in the shadow of the whaler.

She crept cautiously over and looked down at him. It was hardly complimentary to have been mistaken for him. True, he wasn't much bigger than she, but his face was half hidden behind a dirty growth of whiskers. Sandy hoped she'd have nothing to worry about from him for some time. Vaguely dissatisfied, she turned to find a hiding place.

But something stayed her. She frowned in concentration. Yes, that was it! The crew thought it was the watchman who had fallen into the water, but he was completely dry.

When they saw him the others would know it had been someone else in the water, someone else who had climbed up the ladder.

She took a deep breath. Hold on now, she told herself, this is no time to panic, not after coming this far. Then it struck her. If he has to be wet, she decided, then wet he shall be. She crept over and looked down at the prostrate figure. There was, of course, only one way to make him satisfactorily wet—she had to heave him overboard.

The man was almost under the whaler near the edge of the deck so there was no guardrail to worry about. She gave him an experimental push, watching his face. Reassured, she shoved both hands under his body, then with a heave rolled him over. Not quite enough. Once more. The sailor teetered on the edge, then fell right over.

Sandy was already moving towards the shadows when she heard the splash, descending the ladder when she heard loud shouts and curses and a wild thrashing of water. He was wet all right. There was no doubt of that.

Now to find a place to stow away. Familiar as she was with trawlers Sandy had no trouble locating the crew's quarters. She looked quickly around the dimly-lit mess deck. Finally she found a place just opposite the quarters at the foot of the ladder—a small locker with ropes and blocks and fishing gear on shelves. No likelihood of anyone having to come here if they were just returning to Tarbert. It would do.

11

David had lied to Rory. He'd had no other
choice.

He had been brought into the cave at gun-
point. It was a big cave with a heavy curtain
across the back which probably concealed yet
more space. A naked light bulb hung overhead,
powered by a gas-driven generator, and in its
subdued light he saw an electric hot plate, dish-
es, pots and pans, a case of tinned food and several sleeping bags. But these made little impression on him. It was the crew of the *Island
Phantom* that caught his attention.

They were sitting along one wall of the cave,
their bound feet thrust out before them, their
hands tied behind their backs. Rory welcomed
David in a subdued fashion, glad to see him
alive but obviously distraught about his niece.

"Have you any idea what happened to
Sandy?" he asked, emotion making his voice
crack.

And David had had to say no. "She let me

out of the engine room and then the bomb went off. I never saw her after that, Rory. I'm sorry." He winced as he saw Rory's face crumble, but Adam was right there where he would overhear and he must never know the truth.

Adam had made him join the others then, hands and feet bound. No chance presented itself to tell Rory the truth with one guard or another always nearby, so Rory had to remain unaware and in grief all night.

When the trawler had come in David had waited, damp with a sweat that had nothing to do with the warm air, dreading any sound that might tell of Sandy's capture. Later the crew of the trawler had joined Adam and his friends in the cave for a victory celebration. They seemed to have no concern that their festivities might be premature. They were depressingly confident as they settled down to a night of drinking and card playing, having decided that the gale outside was strong enough to delay their trip to Tarbert until morning.

That alone encouraged David. It would give Sandy more time.

He had had a scare when two of the crew had left the cave and shouted to someone on the trawler, but when they came back laughing he was reassured. He gathered that the man left behind on anchor watch had been discovered in the water, evidently the worse for drink. And when a few minutes after returning aboard he had fallen in the water again, their amusement was boundless. Otherwise there was no indication that anything unusual had happened on the trawler. And as the night wore on David became convinced that somehow Sandy had made it.

In the morning—a grey, depressing morning—the *Storvik* finally sailed.

Through the long night of silence David had fretted about Rory, yearning to be able to tell him the truth. His chance finally came when the guard went out briefly to watch the departure of the trawler. For the first time the prisoners were alone.

"Rory," whispered David urgently, "Sandy's alive. She's safe."

For a moment of startled silence, hope and disbelief struggled in Rory's face. "*Tàing do Dhia.* Thanks be to God!" he breathed. "God forgive me for doubting. Tell me, lad, where is she?"

As David hurriedly told him what had happened since the sinking of the *Phantom* Rory's worn features relaxed.

"A miracle, aye, a miracle. Imagine—Conuil's Cave! Do you hear that, lads?" He grinned at the members of his crew, who had been listening intently. "Sandy's on the trawler and she'll bring help. We'll stop these murdering thieves yet. In fact it just may be that we can do our part too. I've been thinking about it all night."

David's pulse quickened. "How?" he whispered.

"Did you see the entrance to the lochan through the cliffs, lad?"

"No, I guess not. I wasn't really looking for it."

"Aye. You can't see it unless you're on the hill opposite. Well, there's a great mass of rock overhanging the channel. It has a deep cleft behind it as if a giant had taken a swipe at it with an axe and almost severed it. A blast of dynamite in that cleft would dislodge mountains of rock into the channel and block it."

"With," said Andra softly, "the submarine inside. Trapped."

"Aye," nodded Rory, "that's the idea. What do you think?"

"Great!" said David. "Theoretically anyway. But where does the dynamite come from?"

Rory nodded his head, pointing. "See the box in the corner over there near the entrance? It's dynamite. I saw it when they herded us in here. I don't know why they've got it here but that's what gave me the idea in the first place."

"But how do we get at it with our feet and hands tied?" asked Seumas.

"I think," said Rory cautiously, "that I have the answer to that too. I've been working at these ropes on my hands all night. They're loose now but I daren't take them right off in case one of the guards checks them. But when the proper time comes—"

"Aye," said the wiry little deck hand, Donald. "I'm almost free too."

"And there are six of us," whispered David, "and only four of them. Three not counting the one at the Peak. If we can overpower them before they get their guns..." His mind raced ahead, visualizing it. "After the submarine is in the loch we block the channel. Then before they can come after us we all head back to Conuil's Cave and safety."

Rory nodded. "But it will not be easy. No doubt they have a signal system and if the submarine doesn't get the correct signal she'll never come in at all. We'll have to wait until she's actually in the loch before we act, if that's possible. Otherwise we could just scare them away and all the Navy will find here will be Adam and the other three men—the submarine and the anthrax bacillus will be out of reach. No, we have to plan this very carefully."

* * *

"What are the plans for that lot?" asked one of Adam's men after returning to the cave from his afternoon post as lookout. He was half-seated on the table casually smoking a cigarette.

"Well," said Adam, "I suppose we should feed them again if they're going to be any help to us in loading the sub." He hefted the kettle, judged it sufficiently full and switched on the hot plate. "The Last Supper for them." He laughed.

Surely Sandy must have reached Tarbert by now, David thought, and contacted Ramshaw. *Please* be on your way here, he pleaded silently.

Adam brought out some bread. "Untie their hands, Tommy," he said. "They can't eat trussed up like that. Don't touch their feet though. And when they're loose keep your gun handy."

David looked quickly at Rory. If their loose bonds were discovered their plan was washed out. Rory frowned and bit his lip.

David's hands were freed first. He rubbed his wrists thankfully.

"You, McCrimmon," Adam ordered. "Come over here. Start spreading some bread."

"Can you loosen my feet then?"

"No. You can hop."

David struggled to his feet, aware that the sailor had turned his attention to Rory. He held his breath, waiting.

"Well," said Tommy. "What have we here? Adam, this one's almost worked himself free."

"Has he now?" said Adam softly. "And what were you hoping to do when you got free, Rory?"

"Hoping to do?" If Rory was discouraged his voice didn't reveal the fact. "Restore circulation in my hands. What else could I do?"

"Nothing," said Adam flatly. "But maybe you didn't know that. All right, Tommy, untie his hands. And when you tie them up again make sure he can't get loose."

David's heart sank. What chance now for their escape plans? He hopped to the table and began to spread margarine onto thick slabs of bread. It was awkward since all Adam had given him to use was a spoon.

"There's not much bread," he said after a moment.

"There are some buns in the box. Use them."

In the dim light David rummaged in the food box. He winced at a sudden stab of pain. What was that? He moved his hand gingerly. A knife! A short, sharp-bladed kitchen knife.

He felt for it again, his hand suddenly sweaty. There. He moved it over beneath the bag of buns.

He glanced nervously over his shoulder. Adam was making coffee. David lifted the bag and the knife and put them on the table in front of him, the knife carefully hidden. As he tore the buns open and spread them he watched Adam out of the corner of his eye. Sure he wasn't being watched, he slid the knife into his pocket and pulled his sweater down over the tip of the handle.

"That's all the buns," he said. He took a handful for the crew and hopped back to his place. He sat down awkwardly, slipped the knife out of his pocket and sat on it. At least there was a chance now.

After they had eaten Tommy tied the prisoners' hands again. Tightly.

It was some time before the crew of the *Phantom* were alone again. Then David whispered, "Rory, I've been thinking. There's still a chance. If your plan is to work we have to wait until the submarine is in the loch before blasting the dynamite. Right?"

"Aye."

"And if we got loose and overpowered the guards too soon the sub would never come in?"

"Aye, that's right but—"

"But if only *one* of us gets loose? Listen. I've got a knife. If I can get it into your hands you can cut me loose. Then I'll take some of that dynamite and get out of here."

"No, I can't let you do that. They would hunt you down—"

"But as long as it's dark they'll never find me. If there's no other way I'll hide out in Conuil's

Cave. They wouldn't warn the sub to stay away just because one man is loose. What can one man do?"

"But when the sub comes in?"

"Will they take time to bother about me? I doubt it. They'll be too anxious to load whatever they're taking with them and get away. I might be able to get the dynamite into that cleft—and they won't harm you until you've got the sub loaded."

"It just might work," breathed Rory. "But I should be the one to go. I've handled dynamite before."

"But you don't know where the cave is. You can tell me what to do with the dynamite. It has to be me, Rory."

"Aye, all right," said Rory reluctantly. "But—Shh. They're coming back."

12

It was late afternoon before the *Storvik* reached Tarbert. When Sandy couldn't figure out why the trip was taking so long she dared a quick look around from the mouth of the hatch leading to her hiding place. South. That meant that the *Storvik* was going all the way around the Uists and then up the east coast again. She knew she would have a long day ahead of her.

Finally the ship's steadying motion told her that they had reached the protecting shores of Loch Tarbert, and at long last the ship slowed into port. Sandy could hear men emerging from the crew's quarters and shouts overhead. The screw churned into reverse. With a slight bump they came alongside the jetty.

She risked a quick look out and was met by lancing rain. The wharf was invitingly close but there were men about and it was still too light. She would have to wait a little longer.

Darkness soon closed in—a thick, heavy darkness. Sandy stood with the door slightly open, waiting for an opportunity to escape. Light streamed from the crew's quarters opposite and there were more lights forward. It was not going to be easy.

Fighting down impatience she waited until the crew seemed to be busy elsewhere, then left her hideout and walked past the open door, checking the impulse to run. She climbed the ladder to the deck and ducked under the lifeboat. For the moment she was in deep shadow but between her and the jetty the deck lay bare in a pale light. Cold rain danced on it in a steady downpour.

Slipping out from beneath the lifeboat Sandy ran swiftly across the streaming deck. She had almost reached the rail when she heard a shout from the bow. She had been seen.

She sprang over the rail to the jetty, racing for a shed that would afford deeper shadows, but before she could reach it a powerful light split the darkness and caught her in its beam. A chorus of shouts spread through the ship. Sandy heard a sharp report and realized with a shock that someone had fired a gun at her.

Then she was around the end of the shed. Briefly she was in darkness, hidden from the trawler. Ahead lay the scattered lights of the village. The rain beat down mercilessly.

She started running down the road. The hard surface jarred her sore ankle so she moved onto the shoulder, but she was beginning to limp. A moment later she stopped again and crouched behind an embankment.

Now what should she do? On the road she would be silhouetted against the village lights. She would have to stay in the ditches until she could reach the shelter of the distant buildings. Then she could get to the hotel and a telephone . . .

Her pursuers had lost her momentarily but now men were coming down the road from the jetty. The glare from their flashlights glinted dully off the barrels of their guns. Sandy began to run again, crouching low. The direction of the voices behind her and the wavering lights told her the men had left the road and were searching the ditches.

She jumped when another shot rang out. They couldn't see her at the moment, she was sure. They must be getting trigger happy. Far down the road a light shone faintly. How far to the hotel?

She skirted a darkened building and thought of breaking in, but decided the men would be sure to look for her there. Keeping low to the ground she ran forward again and ducked between two parked cars just a little past the building. After a moment she straightened cautiously and peered through the windows of the Morris in front of her to look for signs of the men coming down the road. But something in the car itself caught her attention. The keys were in the ignition.

She groped for the door handle. It was unlocked. She squeezed in behind the wheel. How far to Stornoway? Close to an hour, she decided. It meant a little more time before she could contact Ramshaw, but it would get her out of this hornets' nest.

Luckily the engine caught at once and the car shot onto the road. She switched on the lights and the windshield wipers. Rain streamed down over the glass; the road was a dark, wet sheet before her. Suddenly a man appeared in her path, as if from nowhere. There was a gun in his hand.

Flinching, Sandy tramped on the accelerator. The car leapt at the man. The report of the gun tore the stillness. She heard a *thud* as a bullet struck the car somewhere. Then the man hurled himself aside out of her way.

Next turn to the right. She slammed on the brakes as the turn came at her, and the car screeched around the corner. She wrestled with the wheel, then was roaring down the black, streaming road away from the village. She glanced into the rear-view mirror and caught a glimpse of wavering headlights. She was being chased. No one would be driving fast enough to be overtaking her on a night like this, not unless they were trying to catch her. And they *were* overtaking her. She tramped harder on the accelerator. The speedometer needle climbed alarmingly.

She swept over a hill and down a long, curving grade towards what appeared to be a small lake covering the road. At full speed the car plunged into the water, shuddering violently. A curtain of spray shot up in front of Sandy as she felt the smack on the floorboards beneath her feet. She tensed to the drag on the wheel. Then she was through it and starting to climb again. The needle gradually fell back.

As she neared the next crest she spotted a break in the darkness to the right, a sideroad leading off into obscurity. A glance into the mir-

ror confirmed that her pursuers were not yet over
the hill behind. She slammed on the brakes and
twisted the wheel. With a screech of tortured
tires the car spun broadside to the greasy road
and for a moment threatened to overturn. Then
the rear wheels came round and she was facing
the way she had come.

Quickly Sandy changed gears and turned the
car onto the sideroad, which plunged downward
between two steep banks. She switched off the
lights, rolled the window down and stuck her
head out into the stinging rain. She drove a short
distance ahead, then stopped, twisting in her seat
to look back, her heart thumping.

The other car topped the hill and scorched
down the grade. At the bottom of the hill it hit
the water with a resounding *smack*. It emerged
slewing wildly, then steadied on the road and
began climbing. Sandy heard the whine of the
engine as it shot past the sideroad and disappeared over the crest.

In a moment she had backed onto the main
road that headed back towards Tarbert. As the
headlights picked out her skid marks she frowned.
Had her pursuers seen them? If so they would
soon be back. What should she do?

It was too dangerous to go back to Tarbert.
She had a better idea. Somewhere along here was
another sideroad. Not much more than a track in
places, if she remembered correctly, but it turned
off the main road to the west and then veered
northward, eventually coming out on the road
between Stornoway and Calluig. Right near
Ramshaw Castle. And it was doubtful that the

men from the *Storvik* were aware of its existence. It wouldn't be as fast as the highway but that couldn't be helped.

There. A dirt road with no sign marking it. She turned the car carefully, confident that this time the rain would eliminate any tell-tale tire marks. A little way along she slowed down and switched off the lights. For some minutes she crept along with her head out the window so she could see the edge of the road at the front wheel. Gradually she drew away from the highway.

When lights far behind caught her eye Sandy stopped and turned in her seat to watch anxiously. The other car had come back over the hill and now it slowed at the intersection where she had first left the highway. Then it turned off and disappeared.

They wouldn't go far along that road, she knew. She wasn't even sure where it led to—if anywhere. It still wasn't safe to use the lights. She continued to crawl forward in darkness.

It wasn't long before the other car came back. Sandy saw the lights as it turned once more onto the highway and watched it as it roared back towards Tarbert, gathering speed. It swept past the dirt road she had taken and disappeared over the next hill.

She breathed a sigh of relief and switched on the headlights. Her foot pressed down and the Morris lurched forward. How far to Ramshaw Castle? She didn't know. It wasn't as far as Stornoway, but this was a terrible road.

Sandy gasped and stabbed at the brakes as the car dropped away over a sharp crest and swerved from side to side before finally coming to halt, its front wheels off the road. The headlights shone out across the black, rain-lashed waters of a loch. She sat motionless for a moment, her hands shaking on the rim of the wheel. Then slowly she reversed back onto the road and turned the corner. Her foot was lighter on the accelerator. Speed would do her no good if she ended up wrecking the car.

She drove on for what seemed hours, her full attention on the road, bracing herself against the bouncing and bucking of the car, deliberately squelching anxious thoughts and questions about the future. If she didn't keep to the road there would be no future.

She swung the car around a long, water-logged curve. Black mud sucked and grabbed at the wheels. Sandy pressed the accelerator, urging more power, and glanced automatically in the mirror. She was looking away again when something caught her eye—a glow outlined the hill behind. Then the headlights of a car appeared, dancing and swerving down the grade after her. She was being chased again.

She sat on the edge of the seat, urging the car forward, her palms slippery with sweat. How could they travel a road like this at such a speed? The lights behind reflected into her eyes now, blinding her. She turned her mirror away.

The Morris plunged down a sudden grade, took a corner wildly, tightroped along the shoulder—then abruptly the road ended at a crossroad. Sandy jumped on the brakes and spun the wheel. But she was too late—the car shot into the undergrowth on the other side of the cross-road. The wheels slithered, the car lurched. It stopped, tipped precariously, hung there for a moment, then fell over on its side tiredly.

The lights went out; the motor sputtered and stopped. Sandy groped for the flashlight she had noticed earlier under the dash, then reached up and opened the door that was now overhead. She climbed up and out and found herself standing in ragged, calf-deep heather. Rain spread like a wet blanket across everything.

She flashed the light around, peering into the murk. She knew where she was. This was the Stornoway-Calluig Road and Ramshaw Castle was about a twenty-minute walk away.

The lights of the pursuing car swerved behind a low hill. She doused her flashlight, turned and plunged into the black, wet night, running blindly. Wiry stalks of heather were like fingers clutching at her ankles. She stumbled forward, away from the road, while the rain ran into her eyes and streamed down her sodden clothing. At a sudden unseen drop beneath her feet she fell flat. The swollen waters of a brook rushed past, almost at her face.

The car came over the hill. Its lights picked out the overturned Morris. She heard the screech of brakes and the hail of flying gravel as the car shuddered to a stop crossways on the road. Lying where she had fallen, Sandy twisted to watch, her heart pounding.

One man jumped out of the car and ran over to look inside the Morris, then called something to his driver. The car turned so that the headlights reached out into the darkness. The man on the road played a flashlight this way and that.

Sandy didn't move. None of the lights could penetrate far enough to reach her. The pounding of her heart was beginning to ease. She knew they wouldn't catch her now. In the darkness she had no doubt she could evade them indefinitely.

Apparently the two men came to the same conclusion. After a brief consultation and a few more minutes of flashing their lights they drove off in the direction of Stornoway. Sandy watched them go. It was hard to believe they would give up after that mad drive to catch her. Were they really beaten or was this just a trick to lure her back to the road?

She watched until the lights disappeared over a hill. Their glow reappeared farther on, then faded from view. That was reassuring, she thought, but they could still double back with their lights extinguished. She wasn't going to be caught that way.

She headed for Ramshaw Castle. It would have been easier and faster walking on the road, but she could get there by striking across the moor, keeping parallel to the road. And it wasn't far now. If only Ramshaw himself was at home, all her worries would be over.

With occasional cautious probes with the flashlight she walked through the clutching heather, now and then sloshing through streams, sinking into the peaty earth, stumbling over rocks and hillocks, until at last she saw the tower of Ramshaw Castle, a darker shadow rising square and solid in a black world. It was in darkness, at least as far as she could tell. Maybe when she got closer she would see some lights, or maybe it was so late that everyone had retired. She had lost all track of time.

She moved ahead quickly, desperately anxious to see Ramshaw, to end this night of excitement and terror. There was only a tall hedge now between herself and the driveway.

And then a match flared briefly. It was extinguished immediately but it brought Sandy to an abrupt halt, started her heart thumping wildly again. She crouched behind the hedge, peering through. A man was standing silently behind some bushes by the main doors, a cigarette in his hand. And the car that had chased her all the way from Tarbert stood in a grove of trees near the bottom of the driveway.

How had the men guessed that she was headed for Ramshaw Castle? she wondered. How long would they wait around? And where was the second man?

That question, at least, was answered a few minutes later. The sound of footsteps came softly along the driveway. "No sign of anyone on the road. He should be here by now if he's coming."

"I wish I knew who it was," grumbled the man by the doors. "I don't like this at all."

"Neither do I. We're so close to the end." The speaker was a black shadow in the driveway. "But I don't like standing around here either. We don't know how long the others are going to wait for us and it doesn't look as if whoever it is is coming here."

The cigarette glowed momentarily, partially lighting a bearded face. "They won't find Ramshaw anyway. We know that much." That seemed to amuse him. "I don't see how that guy, whoever he is, can have come from Sgeir Dubh. All the prisoners were accounted for. Someone must have come aboard after we got back to Tarbert."

"If so," grunted the other, "he must have been suspicious for some reason. Doesn't make sense either way."

"Sure doesn't. But I don't think we need to worry about him anymore. He's probably wandering on the moor someplace. By the time he reaches civilization it'll be too late."

"He still might show up here sooner or later."

"I know but we can't wait. Look, I'm going inside for a minute to make sure the door into the tower's locked. Then it won't matter if anyone does come. Stand by here and keep an eye out."

Then Ramshaw isn't here, thought Sandy desperately. Have they captured him or killed him? And they must know about that hot-line telephone. Why else would they be worried about the door into the tower? All the same, she decided, I've *got* to get in there. There must be another phone somewhere. I could call *someone*.

But how was she to get in? How, for that matter, was the man going to get in?

Apparently that was no problem. The man took one last drag on his cigarette and flicked it away. Then he took something from his pocket and used it to open the door. It was easy and quick. He disappeared inside.

He'll lock it again when he comes out so I'll be no further ahead, Sandy told herself. I've got to act now. She felt around her feet, found a rock, stood up and tossed it. It fell with a *thud* down the driveway.

The lookout jumped. "Who's there?" He spun around and ran down the lane, groping in his pocket.

Sandy slipped between the hedge and the house and dodged into the open doorway. It was pitch black. Where could she go? She cast her mind back to the day she had come here with David to dine with the Laird. Ramshaw had showed them a cupboard in the hallway, the one that had held his suitcases. Where was it? She felt her way cautiously, her hand groping along the wall.

Somewhere ahead a light flashed briefly. Soft footsteps. Someone was coming.

As she shrank against the wall her hand touched the cupboard doorknob. She turned it carefully and pulled. It opened. A hinge squeaked. She caught her breath, hesitating just a second, expecting the light to blaze in her direction. But it didn't. She slipped inside and closed the door, slowly, gently, not quite all the way.

She stood there scarcely daring to breathe. The footsteps came down the hall and the light flashed again. The man paused at the door, almost within reach. He shone the light around the hall, passing it briefly over the cupboard door. Then he doused it and went outside.

The door closed behind him. Sandy heard the latch rattle as he tried it to make sure it was locked. Then all was silent.

She drew a long, deep breath and let herself out of the cupboard with trembling hands. She went to the door and listened. Nothing for a moment; then voices, indistinct. And at last the sound of a motor breaking into life. She waited, flooded with relief, until the sound receded and vanished altogether.

She stood there for a long moment, shaking all over as the tension eased. At last she switched on her flashlight. The stairs swept overhead into darkness. There was the empty cupboard, a puddle marking the spot where she had stood. The door into the old tower was locked, of course, cutting off all access to the hot line. The one into the library was open but there was no telephone there. She moved around a corner into another hall, her feet squelching on the tiled floor. The kitchen! Maybe there would be a telephone there. And maybe, she thought suddenly, something to eat.

She stopped a moment, listening, but all she could hear was the *drip* of water falling at her feet. It should be safe for lights now.

Sandy ran her hand up the wall by the door and found a switch. Light flooded the kitchen and she blinked in its sudden glare. She switched on all the burners on the stove and leaned over to feel their warmth. Water dripped from her hair and spluttered and hissed on the reddening rings. Maybe in a few minutes she could find a change of clothes. Maybe even have a hot shower. Her eyes brightened at the prospect. But first things first.

She filled the kettle and put it on the hottest burner, then turned and looked around the room. And there it was, hanging on the wall, beckoning. A telephone.

She took the receiver down and cradled it a moment. Now that she was here who was she going to call? The Navy, of course, but how could she get in touch with a destroyer that might or might not be berthed at Stornoway? No, wait. David had told her about an officer, a liaison officer. What was his name? Stanley. Commander Stanley. Now, how could she find him?

Well, there was always the police. She called the operator. "Could you put me on to the police, please. Quickly! This is an emergency."

A voice finally answered. "Hello? Sergeant MacLean here."

"Oh, Sergeant. This is Sandy MacLeod. You know my Uncle Rory, skipper of the *Island Phantom?*"

"Of course. Can I help you?"

"Yes. This is an emergency. I—I have to get in touch with one of the Navy officers right away. A Commander Stanley."

"Was he with the destroyer, Sandy? If so you're too late. She sailed earlier."

The *Audax* had sailed. For Sgeir Dubh? Sandy's hopes rose.

"I'm not positive he'd be on board. He had an

office at the jetty where the *Audax* was berthed but I don't know how to reach it. Sergeant, this is desperately important."

"All right, Sandy. We'll send a car to see if we can find him."

"Thank you. When you find him please tell him to phone me immediately. I'm at Ramshaw Castle. Tell him it's a matter of life and death. Tell him the *Phantom's* been sunk." She heard a gasp at the other end. "I'm sorry, I can't tell you more. Please hurry."

The kettle emitted a piercing shriek. Sandy replaced the receiver. Her hands were still shaking. Would they ever be still again?

She took off the big sweater she had filched from the *Storvik* and hung it over the edge of a shelf where the heat would reach it. Now maybe she could find something to eat. Eggs. And bacon. A frying pan. She hummed in anticipation as the grease sputtered and the aroma began to fill the kitchen. She poured a cup of tea.

The telephone jangled loudly. She ran for it.

"Hello. Sandy MacLeod? This is Commander Stanley."

She breathed a sigh of relief. Thank God. "Oh, Commander, am I glad to hear your voice! You have to send the *Audax* down to Sgeir Dubh right away."

"I'm sorry"—the man was obviously puzzled—"the *Audax* has sailed for the Shetlands. On Ramshaw's orders."

The Shetlands! In the wrong direction entirely! What had happened to David's message to the Laird?

"Perhaps," Commander Stanley said, "you'd better tell me what's going on. The police said something about the *Phantom* having been sunk."

Sandy suppressed her impatience and told him everything. He listened in silence except for a "Good Lord!" when she mentioned the anthrax bacillus. He asked only one or two quick questions when she had finished.

"All right," he said. "I'll get in touch with the authorities immediately and get things moving. Can you stay there by the telephone for a while in case I need to ask you something else? Good. I'll get back to you."

The eggs and bacon were delicious, Sandy decided. Steam rose from her sodden clothing as heat from the stove warmed the kitchen. She needed a change of clothes—or a towel at least—but she couldn't go looking for anything as long as the telephone might ring again.

Was the Navy going to be in time? That was the question. And what time was it anyway? She looked around the kitchen but the only clock had run down. There was one in the library, she remembered. It would just take a minute.

She ran down the hall to the library door and switched on the light. There was the clock. Ten minutes to one. It's already the day the submarine is to arrive at Black Rock Island, she reflected, and then sail away again forever.

The telephone rang. She dashed back to the kitchen and snatched it from the wall. "Yes? Sandy here."

"Sandy, it's Commander Stanley. Look, I just want to set your mind at ease. They failed in their attempt to get the bacillus. It's safe. Ramshaw had an idea someone was after it—he's had extra security over it for the last few days. And today he checked it himself before leaving the building."

"Thank God for that."

"Yes. It's been under foolproof guard ever since. I haven't been able to contact Ramshaw— he left by car and is probably on his way home —but it doesn't matter. Now we just have to figure out how to trap that submarine and net the smugglers. You won't be able to contact me anymore, Sandy, so go and have a good rest and leave everything to us. Your uncle and his crew will be safe and sound in a few hours."

"Thank you, Commander. You're a lifesaver. Goodbye."

Slowly she replaced the receiver. Now she could find that shower and dry her clothes, she thought sleepily. I did it, she said to herself as she poured the last of the tea. Everything is fine.

But why, she wondered, did the tension that had been building up inside her for so long not evaporate? She took another long, deep breath and closed her eyes. Would she never be able to relax again?

Her eyes opened immediately. There was *still* something wrong. Something nagging at her. She rubbed her forehead with a clammy hand. Was there something she had forgotten to tell Commander Stanley? Something vital? Whatever it was had been bothering her for a long time, ever since she had boarded the trawler the night before. Or was it longer than that even? Something that had prodded her again, pestering her, almost breaking through into her conscious mind after she had entered the house. What on earth was it?

She tried to think rationally, to go back step by step. She had run into the house and hid. Where? In that empty cupboard in the hall, the one that had contained Ramshaw's baggage when she and David had first visited the Laird. She remembered it clearly. There had been five blue suitcases.

Her cup crashed to the floor. Five blue suitcases!

She stood there shaking. Suddenly it was all clear—too clear, too devastating.

The men on the trawler had brought the boss's luggage. And they had unloaded five blue suitcases. *Ramshaw!* Ramshaw was the boss! No wonder the *Audax* was heading for the Shetlands—he had sent her up there out of the way. Ramshaw was the brains behind the whole affair. Ramshaw was the man who was in a position to get his hands on the anthrax bacillus. And he had succeeded.

What was it the Commander had said? That Ramshaw had checked it and it had been under guard ever since. What had been under guard—an empty safe?

Ramshaw was away with the bacillus. And there was not a thing Sandy could do about it.

13

Sometime during that long night the prisoners were left alone again. It was time to change the lookout at the Peak and for a few minutes all of Adam's men were absent.

"Now," whispered David urgently. "We may not have much time." He rolled to one side, exposing the knife, and pushed it towards Rory with his bound hands. Rory twisted so his back was towards David. His fingers groped for the knife.

"I have it," he said. "You'll have to back up against me, lad. I hope I don't cut your hands."

David waited tensely. He felt the cold blade touch his skin, was aware of Rory trying to manoeuvre the knife into position. Finally he felt a sawing motion. Then the ropes dropped away.

"Done!" he said triumphantly. He took the knife from Rory and severed the rope around his ankles. After he had rubbed the circulation back into his feet he stood up carefully. "Wish me luck," he whispered.

"Better than that," said Rory. "We'll all be

praying for you. You remember what I told you about the dynamite? Take a look at it. How is it packed?"

David stepped across to the box in the corner.

"Several sticks in a bundle—eight, I guess. And a good length of fuse with each bundle."

"Good. Just take one bundle—more than that will be too awkward to handle in the heather and they'll maybe not notice if there's only one missing. We'll have to hope it will be powerful enough to do the job. You'll need some matches."

"There are some here on the table." And a lighter too, he noticed. He pocketed both. "It'll be wet out there," he said. "What if the dynamite gets damp?"

"Maybe you can find something to wrap it in. Look, there's a jacket over there. Take that. And listen, lad, it's reasonably safe to handle but don't take foolish chances. Hide it somewhere—maybe under a bush or in a cleft in the rock, up beyond the top of the hill if you can manage it. Then you can pick it up later when the submarine has come in. And remember that Sandy's gone for help. We might not have any need for the dynamite."

"I know. I hope not. Well"—he hesitated, waved to them—"I'm off."

Slowly he pushed back the heavy curtain that hung across the entrance. For a moment he paused and listened intently but heard nothing. The bush that grew at the entrance was dripping wet but the rain had stopped. Far overhead was a faint glow indicating that the clouds were thinning, but down below it was very dark. David crept out into the open.

Before him the hill dropped away to the floor of the valley where the lochan lay. Somewhere opposite, he recalled, hidden in the darkness, was the channel that led to the open sea. And overhanging it, according to Rory, a mass of rock.

The hill climbed steeply behind the cave. Off to one side was the Peak. He would have to steer clear of that. Presumably at least two of the men were up there somewhere.

He scrambled up the incline on a diagonal climb to the northwest. From what he could remember of the terrain there should be numerous clefts, bushes and deep heather for temporary hiding places. Good. But first he had to get as far away as possible from the cave.

Out of the corner of his eye he caught the brief flash of a light below. He flattened into the heather and looked back. Two men were approaching the cave, a flashlight now and then glowing, adding grotesque shadows to the movement of their legs.

It won't be long now, he thought. He looked once more towards the Peak but could see nothing. Okay. He had better move while he had the chance.

He scrambled upwards again. Far overhead the clouds were breaking up. Thinner cloud was beginning to turn the sky into a patchwork. If the moon drifted into the areas where the clouds were thin its sheen would outline the top of the cliff. He had to keep below the skyline as long as possible.

Suddenly lights flashed around near the opening to the cave. David could hear shouts and the crackling of a radio. He paused again, crouched in the sopping heather. What were they going to do now?

"Tommy!" a voice barked abruptly out of nowhere.

With a shock David realized there was a radio awfully near at hand, and presumably a man with it. He stared into the darkness but could see nothing.

A moment of silence, then the radio again. "McCrimmon has escaped. Looks like he took matches and a lighter. Maybe he hopes to light a signal fire. He won't . . . " The voice faded away.

The sound seemed to be coming from the direction of the Peak, but certainly not from that distance. Was the original lookout returning? David wondered. Was he coming this way? Looking for him? Of course. They would assume he would go northward where there was more room to run and hide.

What should he do? Wait here in deep shadow and let the lookout get between him and Conuil's Cave or risk being seen now and make a dash for safety? A gust of wind swept across the hilltops. Behind the cloud rack the sky was brightening with filtered moonlight. The deep shadow might not last much longer. He would run for it now.

But first, the dynamite. He would rather have found a cache for it somewhere beyond the hilltop where it could be picked up later, out of sight of anyone down in the valley. But later would have to take care of itself. Right now he needed to run with nothing to hinder his flight.

He pushed the dynamite into the dripping undergrowth beneath a shrub. In the darkness he couldn't see any landmarks that might help him locate it later on, but he had a general idea where he was. That would have to do.

Suddenly the radio crackled again. It was stifled immediately but he could tell it was nearer.

David started running, crouched low. A few minutes later he was almost at the top of the hill. For a short distance he would be in sight of anyone looking his way. He crouched again and glanced up anxiously. It wasn't going to get any darker. He leapt to his feet and raced for the crest of the hill.

He almost made it. A valley was in front of him, its black obscurity beckoning, when a shot rang out. He heard a bullet whine past like an angry hornet.

He plunged downhill, his heart in his mouth. Uneven ground sent him sprawling. He was up again in an instant, running, heedless of bruised knees. It would be a few minutes before his pursuer reached the hilltop. He had to make the most of his time.

Another hill loomed ahead. Once again David would be etched against a lightening sky. But there was no use trying to hide down here in the gloom of the valley; that would be only temporary at best. He climbed, not daring to look back. There were too many rocks and clefts waiting to trip him up to risk even a moment's inattention.

When he knew he would be in view again he began to dodge about as he ran. At least he could be an indistinct target, he thought, and evasive action might increase his chances. In seconds he was into another valley.

The next summit was a sharp one, a steep rock face with a sudden drop on the other side. He struggled up and over and stopped in its shelter to catch his breath. He raised his head cautiously to look back. At first there was nothing to see either in the glen or on the slope beyond. But suddenly three men came over the hill. They were walking openly, slowly, etched black against the sky, spread out at wide intervals. In the increasing glow David saw that two of them carried guns.

Then he realized what they were doing. From here on, the island narrowed until it ended abruptly in a point at the north end. They were driving him northward like shepherds herding sheep into a fold. There was no escape.

At least *they* thought there was no escape. They didn't know about Conuil's Cave.

David turned and ran again. He didn't have to crouch now. The men were confident. They would hold their fire until they had him cornered. He topped the last crest. The final triangle of land lay before him. Beyond it sheer cliffs dropped to the pounding ocean far below. But somewhere beneath the straggling heather at the top was the entrance to the cave.

He spent several frantic minutes trying to locate it. Sweat was running into his eyes and he expected at any moment to hear the cries of his pursuers as they came over the hill and spotted him. At last he found it. Gasping with relief he lowered himself into the cleft.

Then he paused. What would they think, he

wondered, when they came over the hill and found nothing—nothing but rock and heather and the abyss? What *could* they think? Only that he had blundered over the edge. But perhaps he could add a little more reality to the illusion.

They weren't in sight yet but they must be very close. He raised his head a little higher and screamed, a terrified scream. He was still screaming as he lowered himself into the crevice. Then he stopped abruptly. Silence. All the tension of the past few hours had gone into that scream. It must have been convincing, he thought, if his pursuers were close enough to hear it.

He waited just below the surface. A few moments later he heard the sound of pounding feet and shouting voices. Someone stopped so close he could hear heavy breathing. A foot moved the heather an arm's length from his head. He waited, wondering if the man could hear the thumping of his heart.

Then the man muttered, "Bloody young fool!"

Someone else shouted from a distance. The man above yelled back, "Don't go too close. You won't be able to see anything anyway. Just watch you don't join him."

The feet moved away, but not far. A few moments later David heard voices again. "Well, that's that. Must have fallen right over the edge."

"Yeah. He's either dead on the rocks or drowned. Let's get back. It won't be long now."

"Right. In two hours we'll be on our way to a life of luxury. It can't be too soon for me."

He heard more voices, indistinguishable, as the

third man apparently joined the other two. Then the sounds faded. Silence again.

David lowered his body down the cleft and found himself at last in the cave.

He made his way, groping in the inky blackness, out of the inner cave. Two hours the man had said! In two hours they expected to be away in the submarine. He shouldn't have bothered coming down into the cave at all, except it had seemed the only safe place to rest. He would have to get back up there, now that his presence was no longer suspected, to retrieve the dynamite.

Through the tall triangle of the cave mouth he saw the dark, moving mass of the heaving sea, flecked with gleaming phosphorous, reaching ghostly fingers to his feet. A faint glow overhead shone through the thinning cloud. He took a deep breath, welcoming the sting of the salt spray.

Oh, Sandy, he thought, *please* be on your way with some help!

14

Sandy stared at the fragments of her shattered teacup without seeing them. Instead she saw Black Rock Island and a submarine and *HMS Audax* steaming for the Shetlands—and a look of victory on the face of the Laird of Ramshaw.

But there was no need to worry, she told herself. The Navy was still going after the smugglers even if they did believe the bacillus was safe. And there was nothing more she could do about it anyway. Except pray, of course, and she could do that while taking her long-awaited shower.

She went out of the kitchen and down the long hallway, pausing where the wide staircase swept upwards into darkness. She remembered that there was a bathroom about halfway along the hall on the second floor. She had mounted four steps when she stopped short.

From somewhere overhead came a sound, a dull, muffled *thump*. Her heart leapt to her throat. She was not alone in this great, rambling house after all. She stood on the stair, her hand trembling on the bannister. Her eyes automatically measured the distance to the outer door. If she had to run . . .

There it was again, the same muffled sound. It seemed to come from behind a closed door. She stared up into the darkness. Someone was up there. The MacLures perhaps? But if so, what had they been doing all this time? Cowering in their room, afraid to come out, not knowing what was going on?

Thump . . . thump . . . thump. She began to breathe a little more easily. Whatever it was, it didn't sound like someone plotting to attack her, for surely anyone in the house must know by now that she was there.

No, it sounded deliberate. There was a pattern to the noise too. Three thumps in quick succession, three more spaced out and then—Of course! It was Morse code: SOS. It must be the MacLures, she thought, racing up the stairs.

At the top of the stairs her groping fingers located a switch. Light flooded the hallway. She listened intently. For a moment there was silence, then it came again: *thump . . . thump . . . thump.*

Third door along. She stopped outside it, her heart pounding, and tried the knob. It turned but the door refused to open. Then she noticed the key still in the lock. "Hello!" she called. "Who's in there?"

Another moment of silence. Then another series of thumps. She turned the key and pushed against the door. The darkness inside was only slightly relieved by the faint glow from a tiny window. She could just see a shadowy object on the floor.

She found a light switch. In another moment she was kneeling beside the man who lay in the middle of the room, his hands and feet bound, a rag tied tightly over his mouth. One eye stared at her, wide with urgency. She gaped at him.

"Professor Sulsted!" she cried as she loosened the gag. "What in the world are you doing here?"

He licked his lips and tried to speak but couldn't.

"Just a minute," she reassured him. "I'll get you a drink of water. And a knife to cut the ropes."

Sulsted! She had forgotten all about the little man. Ramshaw, of course, had said Sulsted was the brains behind the smuggling operation, but since Ramshaw was apparently that himself...

She ran down the stairs. She could get both water and knife in the kitchen. If the professor wasn't the brains, she wondered as she hunted for a knife to cut the ropes, what was he?

She found out very soon. As she freed Sulsted she told him her story. Then he told his as he paced the floor, gulping food and water between words. "I'm with MI5. Like Ramshaw and Cairns, the man McCrimmon found at the foot of the cliff. Few people know that, of course. Even Ramshaw didn't until I gave myself away by recognizing McCrimmon's feather when he got off the boat at Tobermory."

Sandy stared at him but he silenced her questions with a gesture. "I'm not on this case through the regular channels—that's why Ramshaw didn't know about me. Cairns is the one who put me onto it. He was investigating the

166

submarine rumours on Ramshaw's orders. He learned that smugglers were operating the submarine, running arms to Ireland among other things. He also got a hint that they had something really special in the wind. But he couldn't find out anything more than that and he couldn't get a trace of the leader.

"That's when he started to get suspicious of Ramshaw. He was supposed to be in charge of the MI5 investigation but to Cairns it seemed as if he was blocking it. Cairns knew the smugglers had to be operating out of a base, probably in the Hebrides. But Ramshaw did his best to keep that part of the investigation right away from this area—even McCrimmon saw him doing that."

Sandy nodded. She was beginning to understand what had been happening, except for one thing. "But how do you come into it, Professor?"

"Cairns had a few islands in mind as possible bases—Sgeir Dubh was just one of them. When Ramshaw ordered him to go to the Orkneys to look for a base—an absolute red herring—he realized he needed help. He got in touch with me and told me what he knew. I was to learn what I could about a base and about Ramshaw and he'd try to do the same; then we'd compare notes. We agreed to meet in Tobermory when he got back from the Orkneys. He was to come on the noon boat from Oban wearing a gull's feather so I could identify him—we'd never actually met."

"So you were supposed to find proof that Ramshaw really was leading the smugglers?"

"That's right. I started looking for evidence here in the castle first. I came to call on the

Laird when I knew he wasn't home, hoping to have an opportunity to look around. His man put me in the library to wait, and of course I had to look at the books so he wouldn't be suspicious of me. Lucky I did too because—"

"Because you found the book that told all about Sgeir Dubh. MacLure told us you had been here and must have been the one who read the book." Sandy grinned at Sulsted's look of surprise. "You marked the page and we found it when we were here visiting Ramshaw."

"Yes, I found the book and realized how perfect Sgeir Dubh would be for a base. I was sure it was the right island. But I didn't find anything else in the castle to implicate Ramshaw, just the book itself—which meant that he might also know of Sgeir Dubh's advantages."

"So what did you do?"

"I spent the next few weeks gathering evidence against him. I found enough to prove for sure that Cairns was right about him, and I also began to suspect that the anthrax bacillus might be his special target. That worried me but I had to wait until I met Cairns in Tobermory before I could do anything."

"But then you didn't get to meet him after all," Sandy put in.

Sulsted's face was grave as he nodded. "Ramshaw must have been on to Cairns somehow—had him killed and then intercepted the message McCrimmon got from him. I don't know what Cairns had been able to discover that made him so sure about both the base and Ramshaw even without my information, but when Ramshaw saw the message and then saw me speak to Mc-Crimmon my cover was blown—I didn't notice Ramshaw standing near the lad until I'd already approached him. His men followed me when I left the dock, drugged me and took me aboard the *Storvik*. They needed to find out what I knew and what I had passed along to anyone else."

"And did you tell them anything?" Sandy's voice was tense.

"I figured they would kill me if they found out I had been working completely alone—as long as they didn't know who else might know what I did they were scared and I was safe. Especially when I let them find out I knew about their plan to steal the anthrax bacillus. They had to know if there was likely to be any extra security on it. When they questioned me I was always vague about who else knew of it, so they never felt safe enough to kill me."

"But why are you here now?"

"Two days ago when Ramshaw sent some of his men back here for his precious heirlooms they brought me and left me here. I think they wanted me out of the way while they were busy carrying out the plan, but still alive and available if they ran into trouble and needed a hostage. Remember, they still weren't sure whether anyone was expecting their attack on the bacillus or not. I guess they planned to leave me here forever if they didn't need me. They didn't count on someone like you showing up before they'd completed their escape."

"But what about the MacLures? Wouldn't they have found you? Professor, where *are* the MacLures?"

"Ramshaw's housekeepers, you mean? I've not seen or heard anything of them at all. He must have fired them or sent them off somewhere — or had them killed. They would have caused a lot of trouble if they'd been around to find me, or to report that the paintings and candlesticks were missing, and that's the last thing Ramshaw wants at this stage."

"Candlesticks!" Sandy shook her head. "Is that what he's going back for? It's hard to believe that in spite of all the money Ramshaw's about to make he's taking *them!*"

"Some people," said Sulsted, "are never satisfied. They're valuable family heirlooms and I suppose he couldn't stand to leave them behind."

Sandy had so many more questions she didn't know where to begin. She shook her head to clear it. "So now that I've found you, what do we do?" she asked abruptly.

Sulsted sat down heavily. "There's not much we can do. Ramshaw already has the bacillus—too late to stop that. Thanks to you the Navy is headed for Sgeir Dubh now and I could get MI5 to send in anything I called for. But you see the problem: if anyone gets to the island first the submarine will simply not show up. Ramshaw will just leave his men and valuables there and take off with the bacillus. The Navy has to get there during the few minutes the submarine is in the loch. But how do they do that? A lookout at the Peak could see approaching ships—even air-craft—in plenty of time to get the submarine out and submerged. And in spite of the latest inventions submarines are still hard to detect."

"Still," said Sandy doubtfully, "they *might* locate her and sink her. I suppose that's our only hope now."

"*If* they sink her we've won," Sulsted replied. "I'm quite sure that salt water would destroy the bacillus. But there's little chance of sinking her. If only I could get there before morning," he added.

Sandy looked up at him slowly. "What good would that do?"

He shrugged. "Possibly none. But there might be some way to delay the submarine's departure long enough. Maybe even a few minutes would make all the difference. There would be a chance, however slight. But sitting here there's none whatever."

"Perhaps," said Sandy, wiping her damp palms on her jeans, "perhaps we *could* get out there."

He looked at her, puzzled. "What do you mean? Do you know what time it is? Even if I called MI5 right now it would take a couple of hours for them to get a boat here for me, then more time to make it to the island."

"I don't know what time it is and I don't want to. Do you know Hector MacNeill?"

"Hector MacNeill?" Sulsted frowned. "Oh, yes, I think so. The man with the enormous moustache."

"He has more than a moustache. He also has

the fastest boat in the Islands." Suddenly there was excitement in Sandy's voice. She slid off her stool and started towards the telephone.

"But it's already two in the morning."

"I don't care. And neither will he, I hope. If only I can reach him. He'll do anything for Uncle Rory." She began dialling. "Get ready, Professor. We're on our way."

* * *

"Sandy, lass," bellowed Hector MacNeill, hurrying ahead, "Professor Sulsted. Come aboard, both of you."

Sandy approached the boat cautiously. If Hector piloted it with the same reckless speed as he'd driven his car from Ramshaw Castle she'd be thankful to arrive at Black Rock Island in one piece. Nevertheless, once on board she gave him a quick kiss on the cheek. "You're a marvel, Hector," she said. "I knew we could count on you."

Hector started the engine and the inboard's grumble became a snarl. The boat moved quickly away from the jetty, pitching in the turbulent sea. The stern bit deep, piling the water on either side, churning the wake into a boiling cauldron. The sea swept in over the starboard bow, rolling the boat far over, slapping her down, smothering her in stinging spray. Sulsted went below deck to rest but Sandy stayed on the bridge beside Hector.

"Sandy," he said, after a brief silence, "one question. How are we going to get you two ashore without being seen?"

"By the back door," replied Sandy. "The cave

we told you about. It's in the cliffs at the north end. We'll have to go ashore that way."

Hector looked out the window at the white-flecked sea. "That could be a problem," he said. "There's a chart here with the island on it. Can you show me better where the cave is?" He switched on a light over the chart table and the two of them bent over it.

"There." Sandy put her finger on the spot. "See that point of land? The cave is on this side of it, facing west."

Hector whistled tunelessly through his moustache. "We'll have to bring her about and the sea will be on our starboard quarter, carrying us onto the rocks." He switched off the light and for a moment was lost in thought. "Aye," he said at last, "it will be tricky but we'll manage. Now do you suppose those smugglers will have a lookout on duty?"

"Oh, I'm sure they will. But he'll be on the hill in the southeast part of the island, I expect. We'll have to slow down when we get close, to cut down on our wake. Look at it. They might see that from quite a distance. And our lights. We'll have to black them out."

"Aye, we can do that. Well, lass, there's nothing else to be done for the time being. Why don't you go below too and have a sleep?"

"Sleep?" She laughed. "I'm too wound up for that."

*   *   *

Sandy woke with a start. For a moment she wasn't sure what it was that had wakened her.

Then she realized that the engine's roar had been cut back to a muffled growl. The cruiser no longer crashed jarringly into the waves—she was rolling sickeningly. They must be approaching Sgeir Dubh, Sandy realized, close enough that Hector had throttled right down.

When she emerged onto the upper deck jewelled spume still topped every wind-torn wave, but the subdued wake was quickly dispersing in the writhing sea. The boat was in pitch blackness except for a faint glow up on the flying bridge. There Hector stood at the wheel, peering ahead through the windshield.

"The professor's on the afterdeck," he told her as she joined him. "The fresh air has helped him but he's still a mite weak. I have to go below for a minute, so I'll bring him back with me. Will you take the wheel?"

Hector disappeared, but soon returned with Sulsted in tow. He was carrying two long black rifles. "Here you are, Sandy. Deer rifles and a pair of binoculars."

"Rifles! For goodness sake, Hector—"

"Winchesters!" Sulsted interrupted. "Just what we need. They may not be much against a submarine but I'll tell you, Sandy, I feel a lot more confident with these guns than with nothing at all."

"I'm afraid I have very little ammunition on board," Hector continued. "Both magazines are full—five rounds in each—but that's all. You'll have to use it sparingly. They are in waterproof cases."

"I think we'll be glad of that," said Sandy.

"Aye, you'll be getting wet." Hector had returned to the windshield. "And soon. You can see the cliffs."

A black mass loomed ahead, darker than the black of the sea and sky. Spray flung against it and hung suspended in the air.

"Yonder is the north cliff. We'll bring her about in a few minutes and I'm going to have to turn on the searchlight for a moment when we come around."

"Is that safe?" asked Sulsted anxiously.

"If it's only for a moment I think it is," Sandy replied. "We're well hidden from the Peak. We have to know where the cave is. How's the tide, Hector?"

"It's high now. From what you've told me we'll be able to get in close enough to use a heaving line. I just hope a barbed monkey's fist will catch securely on the rocks."

The boat ran in a little closer, the cliffs looming larger, the *boom* of the surf like approaching thunder. Then Hector made a quick change of course.

They turned into tumbling seas. For a moment the bow was lost in a welter of foam and water engulfed them. Then it lifted and water cascaded off the foredeck. For some minutes they pitched and plunged. The black cliff was on their port side now, stretching out ahead of them.

"It's time to get ready. I'll be bringing her about again in a minute and it won't take us long to run in to the cliff with this sea astern of us."

At his bidding Sulsted and Sandy put on their life jackets. Hector lashed one end of a line to each of them, then handed them the rifles.

The boat was turning again. For a moment she was broadside to the waves, heeling far over. A wave boomed down on the deck above them. Then she was around, heading for the cliffs. The seas rolled in on her starboard quarter.

Hector was shouting at them above the roar of the water. "Away you go to the foredeck now to get the line ashore."

Cautiously Sandy and Sulsted climbed out on the narrow catwalk that led to the bow. Clutching their rifles they clung to the single strand of the guard wire. The spray-laden wind knifed their bodies. They balanced there, shivering, the black mass of the cliff towering above them.

Sandy glanced astern. A huge wave with a boiling crest was bearing down on them. The stern lifted to meet it. She felt herself slipping and grabbed the rail.

The spotlight flashed on. For an instant its finger probed the darkness, picking out a blacker shadow in the dark face of the cliff.

"The cave! That's it!" Sandy cried. On either side of it the breakers smashed against the dark walls.

Sulsted swung his arm and the heaving line snaked out. Then he hauled back on it. "It's caught," he shouted.

The cliffs loomed blacker above them and the waves hurled themselves against the rock, dragging the boat after them. The screws churned desperately against the sea. The boat paused, hung there. The surface was a welter of foam.

"Come on," shouted Sulsted, lashing the end of the heaving line about his waist. He grabbed the rope that tied him to Sandy and together they stepped over the rail. The boat was grinding astern, pulling back from the cliff. Sandy waved to Hector and they jumped into the sea.

The water was surprisingly warm after the cold wind. The waves lifted them and dropped them again and the world was loud with booming surf. Sulsted hauled himself in hand over hand. A wave washed Sandy up beside him, then sucked her away again until the rope between them tautened.

Suddenly there was solid rock beneath her feet. She stood up, knee deep in water, and stared unbelieving at the apparition that stood there regarding her with equal astonishment.

"David!" she cried.

15

A faint light was beginning to show behind filmy clouds when David, Sandy and Sulsted looked down into the valley where the lochan lay. Down there darkness still prevailed, but opposite them the bulk of Lookout Peak was outlined against dawn's first glimmer.

David wasted no time retrieving the dynamite. While the others waited anxiously he crept over the rise and down the slope, checking beneath clumps of still-dripping heather until he found it. In a few minutes he was back with them.

"Okay," he said in a low voice. "Now let's go over the plan again."

"You two take the dynamite and one rifle and get over there near the channel. I stay here in reserve." Sulsted sounded less than happy with his own role.

"It's the best way," said Sandy. "We know the lay of the land and you're still weak after being tied up for so long. Besides, we need you here, Professor. You're the most experienced with a rifle and when Uncle Rory and the crew have finished loading the sub I doubt Adam will lose much time before finishing them off. You have to be here ready to move in as soon as you sense the men are in danger."

David agreed. "You'll just have to play it by ear. For instance, if the dynamite doesn't do the job—"

"All right," said Sulsted. "We'll worry about that if it happens. I'll be here to cover your retreat anyway. You had better go while it's still dark. You have to pass pretty close to that lookout."

"Right." Sandy touched his arm, then turned. "Let's go, David." She hung the strap of Hector's binoculars over her shoulder and picked up the rifle. David carried the dynamite and a rope.

The first part was easy. They hurried along the curving hollow that took them around the valley. A rise on the left hid them from the man at the Peak. As they drew near the highest hill the sheltering rise disappeared and only sloping ground lay between Lookout Peak and the cliff top. David put a warning hand on Sandy's arm and side by side they flattened into the dripping heather and waited, their eyes on the Peak.

In a few moments the lookout appeared. They watch him searching through his binoculars to the south, the west over and beyond where they lay, the north, the east and back again slowly. Finally he paused, lowering the glasses and rubbing his eyes. He stood there for some moments, then moved off to the other side of the hill.

In the gradually increasing light David had spotted the dark shapes of some rocks ahead.

"Let's make for those," he whispered. "We'll wait there for his next turn."

Sandy nodded. They rose, stooped low and ran over the uneven ground. In a short time they lay full length among the rocks.

The lookout reappeared. With dawn stretching out pale fingers his duty took on new meaning. Where before there was unrelieved darkness, he could now see the grey sea merging with the sky, the far shapes of other islands. Had he looked down he might have wondered at the altered shapes of the shadows cast by the rocks. But if danger was to come at all, he knew, it would be from the sea or the air.

They were at the end of the island now. Here there was just a high, narrow rim between the valley on one side and the Atlantic pounding the base of the cliffs on the other. Then the rim broadened out as it curved eastward, finally culminating in the mass of rock overhanging the channel.

As soon as the lookout disappeared Sandy and David were on their feet again, crouched low and running. They stopped where the thick undergrowth deepened. They were approaching a point where they would no longer be hidden from the lookout when he was pausing between sweeps. But the undergrowth was more abundant here and as the rim broadened out low hills afforded added cover.

Daylight had taken command when Sandy and David looked down into the loch from a point not far from the overhanging mass. A rise of ground hid them from the Peak and rocks and heather provided closer shelter.

"Now we wait for the submarine."

"I hope it's a long wait." Sandy gratefully set the rifle down and lay beside it. "The later it comes the better the chance the Navy will be here in time. Maybe we won't have to mess around with that dynamite." She looked at the package David had so carefully nursed across the island. "Do you think we should get it down into position now?"

He shook his head. "Plenty of time for that. We can wait till the lookout leaves his position to go down and board the sub. It'll take him five or ten minutes to get there and that's more time than we need. That way we won't have to worry about him seeing us."

"Yes, that's good." Sandy took the binoculars from around her neck and propped them on a rock in front of her. She pillowed her head on her arm and yawned widely.

"If you can sleep now you're either a pretty cool customer or you're about dead on your feet."

"As you may have noticed I'm not on my feet, but I think I *am* about dead. I had only a short nap on Hector's boat last night and I don't remember when I slept before that. Wake me in half an hour and you can take your turn."

David chuckled as he picked up the binoculars. In no time Sandy appeared to be asleep beside him.

Suddenly he jerked to attention. Adam Brieve had emerged from the cave in the hillside with a steaming cup in his hands. He waved casually in the direction of the Peak, then paced aimlessly, alternately drawing on a cigarette and drinking from his cup.

When both were finished he disappeared again for a few minutes, then returned carrying his rifle. He stood beside the mouth of the cave as the men from the *Island Phantom* came out one by one.

Rory appeared first. David saw him look all around, first down into the bottom of the cupped valley, then around the rim of circling hills. Hopefully, David thought. He'll be hoping that Sandy made it safely to Tarbert to get help and that I didn't really fall over the cliff.

Behind Rory came the rest of the crew. Under the threat of Adam's gun they began to move cases and bundles of various sizes from the cave to a dinghy at the water's edge—including five blue suitcases.

David felt a hand on his arm. Sandy was there beside him, yawning. He handed her the binoculars.

"There they are," he said. "Five blue suitcases. I remember seeing them in Ramshaw's cupboard when we visited the castle, but I didn't recognize them when they were unloaded off the *Storvik*. It's a good thing you did."

"It took me a long time," she admitted. Then she added softly, fiercely, "He'll be sorry. Oh, won't they all be sorry!"

"I hope so. But I guess they're not worried right now. They're getting ready to leave in triumph."

As they watched, Adam removed his walkie-talkie from its pouch, adjusted the antenna and spoke into it, then turned and waved towards the Peak.

"Something's up," said David. "I'm going to move over a bit so I can see what the lookout's doing."

"Be careful."

He wormed his way back among the rocks to a position from which the rise in the ground no longer hid Lookout Peak from view. The lookout was standing up, his glasses to his eyes. David watched as he made a long, careful sweep around the island. He paused for a long time gazing northward and David wondered, with quickening pulse, if he had spotted a ship heading in their direction. He completed the sweep, then turned the glasses northward once again. But whether he simply saw something of interest or assumed that if danger were to threaten it would be from that direction, the man was apparently not worried. He let the glasses drop and dangle on their strap as he stood looking down into the valley.

A movement caught David's eye. Sandy was beckoning to him excitedly. He worked his way back to her.

"It's here," she said. "The submarine's back." He looked down over the edge of the cliff and saw it nosing through the channel below them, water rolling off the rounded hull.

He wiped a sweaty hand across his brow. There she was—in the trap. It only remained for them to spring it.

The submarine moved silently across the loch.

Men stood on her bridge and more appeared on deck, talking together casually, waving to those on shore. She nosed in towards the beach, then stopped with a swirl of green water at the stern. Quickly two men jumped into the loaded dinghy and headed towards the ship.

David was aware that Sandy had tensed beside him. "David, look. On the bridge. That's Ramshaw, isn't it?"

It was Ramshaw all right, standing there on the conning tower bridge. David nodded slowly. If there had been any doubt about Sandy's accusation of the Laird it was gone now. He remembered when Ramshaw had sat beside him on the *Skerryvore* and casually mentioned the name of John Edward Cairns, the dead man. He remembered the air of competence and how it had reassured him, effectively putting an end to the moment of doubtful surprise at his appearance there on the *Skerryvore* instead of at dockside in Tobermory.

"There goes the lookout. I hope Professor Sulsted's got a close watch on Uncle Rory and the crew," said Sandy fervently. "We'd better get the dynamite into position."

"Right. Let's go." Together they moved out from their cover and ran across the hill until they were above the cleft that almost severed the overhanging mass.

"Okay," said David. "Rory told me what to do with this stuff so I'll go down. There should be plenty of rope." They were using the line that had lashed Sandy and Sulsted together on their watery landing from Hector's launch. "Lower the dynamite and try not to let it bump against the cliff. I prefer to climb back up under my own steam!"

It was a sheer drop into the cleft but the scarred face offered numerous handholds and plenty of wiry roots grew out from the cliff. David lowered himself over the edge, seeking out supports as he needed them until he was deep in the fissure. He fell a short distance when his fingers lost their grip but there was no time to wonder if he had hurt himself. The bundle of dynamite sticks was there ahead of him. He removed the rope and strung the fuse out along the ground.

David looked up and saw Sandy above him, watching activities that were beyond his view. He pictured the submarine ready to move across the loch. Adam Brieve and the Laird of Ramshaw would undoubtedly be supremely confident now as Black Rock Island was about to drop out of their lives. In a few minutes they would be heading out to sea on their way to a new life of luxury.

Now! Sandy's hand chopped down in an unmistakable signal.

He knelt down, using his body to shelter the lighter from the wind that whistled through the crevice. The fuse sputtered, then caught. The tiny red glow began to move slowly towards the dynamite. Agonizingly slowly.

Three minutes. That was what Rory had said. It seemed more like three weeks.

"Davie! Hurry up out of there, for goodness sake!"

The urgency in Sandy's voice startled him. Suddenly realizing the danger he was in, he sprang away from the dynamite, grabbed at a gnarled root growing out of the cliff face above him and sought for a crevice with scrabbling feet. The root came away in his hand and he fell back.

Immediately he was up again, aware of a pain in his hip. But there was no time for that. He cast an anxious eye at the fuse. All at once the red spark was travelling at an alarming speed.

Taking a deep breath to calm himself he found crevices for his feet and fingers and lifted himself up. Slowly, deliberately, he tried each handhold before trusting it. He climbed steadily, ignoring the smouldering death below, until Sandy's hand was there to help him. She pulled him up and together they rolled away from the edge of the cliff. They started running.

"Okay," David panted as they topped a small rise. "We should be safe from the blast now. I'll see what's happening."

His heart pounded as he stood looking down into the loch. The submarine had been loaded. Rory and his crew were being herded back away from the shore. In another minute or two it would be too late. They would be disposed of and the sub would thread her way through the channel to freedom.

But there wasn't another minute. The cleft above the submarine belched an orange flame and a great burst of yellow smoke. A roar, full-throated and deafening, reverberated over the hilltops. A blast of hot air swept up and back, flinging David off his feet. He fell hard and went rolling uncontrollably down the slope. Pieces of rock and dirt rained around him.

For a moment everything was blank. Then he found Sandy leaning over him, brushing dirt off his face. There was blood on her fingertips. "You're hurt," she said.

David shook his head, then remembered where he was. He struggled up and again looked down into the loch.

The submarine was dead in the water below them. Great pieces of rock lay on her battered foredeck. Bewildered men were shouting back and forth and staring upwards. One seaman lay motionless. Adam and two others, no longer concerned with disposing of Rory and the crew, were in the dinghy frantically making their way towards the sub.

David turned and grabbed Sandy in the exultation of victory. "We did it!" he cried. The trap had been sprung.

But Sandy shook her head. "We didn't. We *didn't. Look!*" She pointed down into the channel.

David looked and his heart sank. The plunging rock had been swallowed up by the water below. The channel was still open.

He glanced at his wrist in despair but there was no watch there. "What time is it?" he yelled. "Where the blazes is the Navy?"

"I don't know," Sandy said hopelessly. "It's too late now anyway. As soon as the sub gets through the channel she'll submerge and they'll never find her." She sighed. "At least we made them forget about Uncle Rory—thank goodness for that. But we've as good as let the sub get away."

They were lying side by side now, peering over the edge of the cliff. The submarine was moving again, slowly. Ramshaw and Adam were standing together at the stern, anxious, uncertain about what had happened. Other men stood about on the deck, several of them on the bridge, raking the cliff top with binoculars. And on the bow three men were peering into the water ahead.

"Where's the rifle?" growled David, his dismay turning to anger.

"You won't stop a submarine with a deer rifle."

"It's all we've got. If we can just delay them a little longer—"

"Yes!" said Sandy suddenly, tensely. "If only we can delay them. Look at the cliff, Davie. See that crack? More of the rock face has been weakened. I think it's going to go!"

He nodded slowly. He could see a new rift that hadn't been there a few minutes ago and it seemed to be widening. We watched till his eyes ached. "It had better hurry and do something," he said anxiously. Deliberately he turned away, hardly daring to hope, and looked back at the submarine.

One of the men at the bow held a rope with a sinker on the end of it. He twirled the rope once like a lariat, then let the heavy end fall into the water ahead of the sub. At frequent intervals he pulled it up and examined it.

"What's he doing?" David asked.

"Sounding the depths. They don't know if they

have enough clearance to get over the rocks."
Suddenly she pushed the rifle towards him. "Aim
at those men, Davie. If we scare them off they
might be afraid to move through the channel in
case they tear the bottom out. Have you ever
fired a rifle?"

He shook his head.

"I have," she said. "At a target. But I never
fired at a man before. I hope I don't hit one."

She took the gun back and fired once. She
came close—too close for the men in the bow.
They started a hurried retreat towards the conning tower but Ramshaw yelled something at
them and waved them back. Suddenly there were
men beside him with automatic machine guns.

"Let's get out of here," said David. "I don't
like the look of those things."

As they dropped down behind the crest they
heard one of the machine guns stutter with a
loud, steady bark. Bullets pummelled the cliff
and chunks of rock leapt skyward.

Sandy and David crept forward to a new spot,
away from where the guns had scarred the rock
face, and risked another look over. The smoking
guns were silent as the men searched the cliff top
for some sign of their unexpected foe. And the
nose of the submarine was now over the submerged barrier, moving carefully.

The crack in the cliff face was still there too,
like a petrified jag of black lightning. David was
staring at it, willing it to expand, when Sandy
clutched his arm and pointed.

On the afterdeck of the submarine a hatch had
opened. A deck gun was rising smoothly into

view. It settled into position while men took up stations around it. The muzzle was lifting, sniffing the air.

"What's that thing?" gasped David.

"It's huge," said Sandy, awed. "But surely they're not going to fire that great ruddy thing at us. They're just trying to scare us. They don't know who's up here or how many or anything. A shell from that ... " Her voice trailed away.

Then all at once she was excited. "Maybe they *will* fire it. Where's the rifle, Davie? I've got to shoot again. We've got to make them mad."

He stared at her. "You *want* them to fire that monster?"

"Yes!" She pointed to the cliff looming above the creeping submarine. "The crack! Look, it's getting wider. Maybe the concussion from that gun is all we need. It's our only hope now."

She raised the rifle to her shoulder and began to shoot. Finally the magazine was empty. But it was enough. A shell was rammed into the breech of the deck gun and the muzzle was pointed right at them.

"All right," said David calmly, "let's go."

They fled. The bulk of Lookout Peak was behind them when the gun went off. An ear-splitting thunderclap rent the air, echoing and reechoing across the hills. Beyond the Peak they saw a flash, then a cloud of smoke and debris. Rock and earth erupted skyward.

From a new position well away from their former vantage point they looked once more towards the loch. Wreaths of smoke still feathered from the muzzle of the deck gun. The gun crew and the men on the bridge were searching the rim above them. The men in the bow were still peering over the side of the sub as the rocks slipped away below. At the stern Adam and Ramshaw, hands clasped over their ears, watched as the submarine entered the channel. The freedom of the open sea lay only moments ahead.

Then Sandy caught David's arm. "Look," she breathed, awe-struck. "Look at that."

The jagged cleft was widening. Slowly. Painfully slowly.

Then someone on the submarine saw it. They heard him scream and saw him pointing at the cliff. The screw churned the water desperately in one last effort to escape, but it was too late. The sailors stood motionless, helpless as death loomed above them.

The whole cliff face was bulging out, moving. It started in slow motion with a low rumble. Then the rumble became a voice of thunder. The vast mass of the cliff gave way and smashed into the channel. It struck the submarine. Amid a tidal wave of wild water and a great cloud of flying rock and debris the stern jacknifed, hurling the two men there high into the air.

When the water and debris settled most of the submarine had disappeared, crushed beneath a mountain of rock. Only the stern remained, canted crazily, the twin screws, obscenely exposed, beating feebly against the air.

The only sign of life was two men floating in the seething water. Ramshaw and Adam had survived to face the consequences.

*   *   *

The Navy came by both air and sea.

Sandy and David were still gazing in awe at the submarine when a helicopter swept in over their heads. It circled, hovering, then settled on the shore of the loch. At the same moment, far out to sea they saw a warship approaching. Its bow wave creamed and curled, occasionally washing the ship in flying spume.

Hand in hand Sandy and David made their way to the shore where they were greeted with delirious acclaim by Rory and the crew of the *Phantom*. Professor Sulsted had climbed down from his vantage point to join them. Commander Stanley stood beside the helicopter with a broad grin on his face.

Two other men stood there also, a little apart. Unguarded, dripping wet, defeated.

Adam's single black brow was lowered over brooding eyes. He said nothing. Ramshaw saw Sandy and David. He made a mock bow. Then he held out one hand, the thumb and forefinger just a little apart. "We were that close!" He shook his head in disbelief. "And do you know what hurts? We were beaten by a couple of kids!"

* * *

"A couple of kids! How do you like that?"

Sandy and David stood at the stern of the destroyer beneath the shadow of the guns. Back beyond the ship's seething wake the birds still swarmed about the heights of Sgeir Dubh.

Sandy laughed. "It shows what a couple of kids can do when they call in expert help. I never prayed so hard in my life."

David caught the dancing light in her eyes. "You know," he said, "I think you really enjoyed it."

She pondered that. "Parts of it," she admitted. "There were good times, like when I met you on the jetty in Tobermory. But all things considered—"

"It wasn't worth it. Is that what you were going to say?" He laughed. "How would you like to meet me again? Under normal circumstances. I live about as far from an ocean as you can get and there isn't a cave in sight. You and Rory would enjoy a holiday there."

Sandy shook her head. "Uncle Rory wouldn't— you couldn't drag him away from his Islands, even for a vacation. But I just might consider it. After all the excitement of the last few days a town with a cow as the local heroine sounds very attractive."

David nodded, pleased. "Consider it. That's all I ask."

Together they watched Black Rock Island fade into the distant blue haze until they could no longer see it.